The Painted Catch

THE PAINTED CATCH

RONDER SCOTT

TENTH STREET PRESS

THIS EDITION

© Copyright 2014 Ronder Scott

Published by Tenth Street Press 2014

Cover design by Axel for Tenth Street Press

ISBN-10: 0-9923861-7-9

ISBN-13: 978-0-9923861-7-7

PRINTED IN THE U.S.A.

TENTH STREET PRESS Ltd.
MELBOURNE LONDON
www.tenthstreetpress.com
Email: contact@tenthstreetpress.com

CONTENTS

Chapter One:
A Platoon's Mistake

Shane Braff sat on the floor, staring at the television screen, watching a pre-recorded tape of Tayyip Nafisi's house in horror. He looked at his young, innocent daughter Emily, who was staring at the picture, entranced by it and with a wrinkled brow, showing she didn't quite understand. Yet she didn't blink, her eyes remaining frozen as she stared at the screen, seemingly unable to turn away. He wanted to yell out for her to look at him, but he was unable to speak.

Finally his daughter spoke without turning around. Emily asked, "Is that you, Daddy?"

He couldn't answer. His head began throbbing and he felt the sweat beading up on his forehead, disgusted by what he saw and revolted by the haunting memories of that day. His mind went into a tailspin. Staring at a picture that wasn't as vivid as the incident was in his mind when it went down.

Four soldiers dressed in uniforms, one Captain and three MPs, were knocking on the door to a modest home in Afghanistan. The door swung open and a man looked at them casually, waiting for them to say what they needed. It wasn't uncommon for the military to scout the area, looking for those who were hiding from the U.S. troops.

Captain Issac Rainnek identified himself and spoke.

"Mr. Taan Latif?"

Tayyip Nafisi, the man who answered the door replied. "No...no sir."

"We have reason to believe you are Taan Latif." Rainnek handed the man a copy of a photo and then continued talking. "Request to enter premises."

There was no waiting for a response. With a bully mentality and no signs of hesitation, MP Lieutenant Shane Braff and the two MPs under his command pushed open the door. They told Tayyip to get down and he immediately complied, kneeling on the floor with his hands on the ground, commanded not to move. The photo was still clutched in his hand.

"Please spare my life," he begged, staring at them with large brown eyes that were frightened, yet still managed to show hints of anger. "This is not me. I am not this man you are seeking."

Shane said, "Fuck it man. Fuck this shit! That's him. We all know it is. I say let's take him out now!"

"No, he still has to be detained," Captain Rainnek commanded.

Shane was shaking from that adrenaline rush that came from knowing he had the opportunity to wipe out a terrorist SOB. His finger went to the trigger of the gun and Rainnek turned his head away from Shane, knowing he'd stated what he must. The rest was...well, out of his control. Shane moved a step closer, his heavy boots making loud thuds on the linoleum of the entry way, and with his M-16 rifle he shoved the muzzle of it in Tayyip's face.

"Papa!" Hossien screamed. The small boy ran over to his father and tried to shove the soldier away, desperate to do what he could to save his papa. "Leave him alone!" He turned to the four American soldiers, no fear in his eyes, and tried to stand his ground despite being a fraction of their size and having no weapons other than his words.

The response was a jab in the chest with the butt of a gun that sent the young boy flying backward. Nobody dared to move to come to the boy's rescue for fear of their own lives. Dan Markel turned to Tayyip and punched him in the face, sending his body flopping down to the side from the impact of the punch. Flecks of bright red blood splattered the soldier's hand and went flying through the air in slow motion, landing on the white walls and linoleum, and rippling out, looking like a pebble that had just skimmed a lake. Then Markel sneered as everyone looked horrified, terror showing in their eyes.

Faridah Nafisi, a beautiful Iraqi woman, tried to reach out toward her husband, but was held back in the room by the other two MPs. "We are American. I can show you my passport. Please sir, please." Markel looked at her before taking two steps to cross the room to get to her. When he grabbed her arm, his instincts kicked in. He made sure she wasn't armed with any weapons and forced her to remove her burqa, revealing a thin frame and firm uplifted breasts that didn't look like those of a woman who'd birthed a child.

Tayyip grabbed at his hair, not concerned about what was his own well-being. On the ground, he pled for the soldiers to show mercy on his son. "Please let me help my son. He can't breathe. He has asthma. He must have his inhaler...please." His words were desperate pleas from a frantic father who loved his only child dearly.

Dan, the one who delivered the swift punch to the jaw, said, "No...you stay there." He kicked Tayyip in the ribs to ensure his prisoner did as ordered. Once the man was properly cowed, the soldier walked over to the boy and placed him on his side. The child was gasping for air. Markel stared at him, showing no emotion what-so-ever for the boy who was struggling to breathe. Hossien's face showed the desperation that came with not having enough oxygen to survive. Markel continued to stare, as if the young boy was lying. Then it was too late to do anything. Shortly thereafter, Hossien drew his last breath. His parents were left screaming and crying, begging for mercy, wondering how anyone could have let such a thing happen.

Their screams went unanswered. Instead, the response was cuffing Tayyip's hands tightly behind his back and pulling him upright but he didn't stop shouting. Even as a prisoner, he called out to his wife, tears streaming from his eyes.

As he was led out of the room, he stopped briefly,

staring at the lone female soldier. She was just sitting on the floor and shaking. While she had done nothing to physically harm them, her lack of action resulted in the hurting and killing of his family. She knew it and when she caught the forlorn father staring at her, she knew he sensed it too.

Jennifer Koppell was sitting on the floor. Her hands were covering her mouth as tears flowed from her eyes. She cringed at the painful look in the man's eyes and quickly turned away, breathing deeply as the room began spinning around her, leaving her standing still in time -- stuck in place.

Dan Markel drug Tayyip to another room, making it impossible for him to walk because of the difference in stature between the men. The soldier began to strip Tayyip's shorts off, turning him over on his side afterward. Braff followed him into the room with a whip that had a noose connected to the end of it. They secured it around his neck and dragged him out of his house, going past his exhausted and collapsed wife, and into his front yard where the military van waited. He was defeated; he was humiliated. He saw neighbors staring at him through small cracks in their curtains, fearful of being the next target of the soldiers.

Tayyip and three of the four MPs were out in the vehicle waiting, but Jennifer was still inside, unable to move and completely unsettled from everything. She was completely shaken and disturbed by what she'd just witnessed.

Chapter Two:
Guantanamo Bay Prison

The General was trying to gloss over a critical error that had been made by the US military and the squad of soldiers that had been among their best. Despite their past records of exemplary service, their recent actions were unacceptable and possibly costly. "I want to apologize on behalf of my men for what happened to you, Mr. Nafisi. It is a true case of mistaken identity. My soldiers had been misinformed and the one you were mistaken for was of great concern to our security. I know it doesn't ease the pain of your loss, but we do accept responsibility. We give you our apology with genuine sincerity. I know it can't change what happened, but we are offering you a full pardon and a new start. You're free to go as soon as we get all the paperwork done."

Tayyip sat in a chair facing the man silently, not bothering to express what was in his heart. This man was only worried with covering his ass and his country's ass, not in truly making amends for a wrong. He stared at the Captain General contentedly, devoid of all expression. "What will happen to the soldiers who did this?"

"They will be punished."

"How?"

"Through the proper military channels," the General replied.

Two hours later, Tayyip nodded his head, staring down at his khaki pants and plucking a small piece of lint from them. He was wearing a collared shirt, neatly pressed and hanging loosely over his frame. He wore another shirt over his head, hiding his face from the scrutinizing gaze of prisoners and soldiers alike as he passed through the high barbed wire fence. That fence symbolized the short distance between a man's freedom and his enslavement, but he was glad to be leaving. As the gates slid closed behind him, he heard the sounds of the automated locks, electrical currents that surged through them, and the tough steel surrounding it all. Now it was time for Tayyip to look ahead. He started into the Cuban sand drifts in front of him and walked slowly, seeing the sun shining down brightly.

Not daring to turn around and stare back at the prison to his physical body, Tayyip left the American compound in the distance. He knew he was physically free, but he was still trapped in a mental prison that showed no pardon in the foreseeable future.

Once back home in Afghanistan, Tayyip's wife, Faridah, could only stare at her husband. She wasn't sure how to handle his presence and she was still struggling to handle her son's death. Tears were running down her face as the sounds of guns outside echoed everywhere, making her cover her ears in anguish. She was tormented, ruined.

Wanting to escape the anguish, Faridah went into the bathroom and shut the door softly. As she began filling up the bathtub with steaming water, she let her hair down. She stripped off her clothes and walked over to the mirror. Her eyes studied her features as if she had never looked upon herself before. She looked sickly, like she was half dead, perhaps even the undead. Her home was her tomb, a place where couldn't escape because it was just too much of an emotional burden to be anywhere else.

Faridah slid her slight frame into the tub, submerging herself in the warmth. She hoped it would help to numb her pain and give her a reprieve. There was a soft knock on the door. She didn't call out or look toward it. Instead, she turned her head to the tile wall in the bathroom.

Tayyip walked over and leaned down to his frail wife, kissing her forehead gently. "I wish there was something I could do."

Faridah's voice was devoid of emotion and bland. She asked, "Why did we come back here?" Then she put her bony arms, no bigger than those of a child, up to her chest and began to pound, slamming on it as if she was trying to get her heart to beat. The tears were flowing down her face as she released the pain that she struggled to keep hidden, locked away because it was so damn hard to deal with.

Tayyip said, "Please." He grabbed her hands, trying to get her to stop pounding on her bony chest. His efforts to calm her were futile.

She screamed. "Get out!"

Just then the house shook, feeling like the ground was opening up to swallow the dwelling. There was no earthquake though. The house was shaking from being hit by yet another shell, gunfire from the battles that frequently took place in the streets without warning. The mirror above the sink swayed back and forth. Finally, it fell off the nail it was on. It went crashing onto the floor, sending shards of broken mirror pieces across the tile, creating an erratic mosaic. Her foot had been dangling over the edge of the tub and one of the shards flew through the air, landing on it and cutting her. Blood ran down her foot to the bone of her ankle, trickling down onto the floor.

Tayyip immediately tried to help. "Let me," he said gently.

"Just stop."

"Listen, you know as soon as they give us our passports back we can re-enter the States. We'll be able to leave here…start new and put all this pain behind."

Faridah showed more expression than she had since Tayyip's return. "My Hossien will never return. My pain will never be gone!" She stared at him, looking at him like he was the evil one, the one that had stolen her life away from her. A sigh shook her entire body. "I told you not to come back over here, but you wouldn't listen. Now our son is dead and you can't bring him back." She retreated to the corner of the tub and hugged her knees to her chin, looking like a small infant that was ready to rebel against their parent.

Not knowing how he could connect with his wife any longer, Tayyip resigned to the fact that he was not helping. He gave up and retreated to the kitchen to get something to clean up the glass.

He came back with a plastic bag and a broom. The door was halfway open and he could see the small stream of blood had grown, going between the cracks of the tile floor and spreading themselves through it like a snake would slither through the pipes of a home or sewer.

His heart race. He heard no cries or noises of any sort. His heart hoped that she'd stopped weeping, but as he swung open the door, he knew that was not the case. The soldiers killed her, just as they killed Hossien.

Faridah's body was slouched over the edge of the tub. A large shard of glass rose from the middle of her thigh like a tower. The stream of blood that flowed from the femoral artery spilled onto the floor. Tayyip immediately knew that this deep wound was one that could not be mended with any amount of medical attention.

A loud knock sounded out at the door, making Tayyip jump. From all he'd been through, he instantly felt guilty despite doing nothing at all. He ran to the door and opened it up, feeling numb.

When he opened the door, he saw a US soldier in a long sleeve camouflage uniform, tailored with red and gold on the pocket and sleeve. He held a certified letter. Soldier Fred Camen said, "Are you Tayyip Nafisi?" All

Tayyip could do was think back to the day it all started: four soldiers at his door, dressed in uniform and asking if he was Mr. Taan Latif. It hadn't mattered that he wasn't. They'd crashed through that door anyway and changed his life forever. He'd gone from a man with a loving family to a man who was all alone.

"Sir, are you Tayyip Nafisi?" the soldier repeated.

"Yes, that's me."

"This letter is for you." Tayyip reached out and took the letter from the soldier's extended hand, not even looking at the man. The soldier just replied, "Thank you. Have a good day, sir." Having completed his duty, the soldier turned and walked away.

The letter gave him freedom, but it didn't make up for the fact that it also acknowledged that his life had been stolen from him unjustly. He walked back to the bathroom and began to clean it up. When he was finished, he removed Faridah's body and lay it on the bed. He dressed her in a white see-through gown that covered her to her ankles. She looked lovely and angelic, so pure and rid of the demons that had tortured her so much the past years.

Tayyip put candles around the room and lit them all, allowing them to burn into the night. He leaned over his wife, applying make-up to her face so she looked like a sleeping angel. She was lying there so peacefully that he couldn't stop staring. He mourned her loss alone, knowing that no one else cared or could be there to comfort him. There was no human touch of comfort to be offered to him. All he had for company were the thoughts of what had been stolen from him. Faridah had been incredible, someone he had loved from the first minute he'd ever laid eyes on her.

That night, Tayyip slept on the floor of the room in which he mourned his wife. Not wanting to leave her side, he held his hand up on the bed, touching hers gently so she would know that she was not alone. Equally, he also needed to feel that he was not all alone for the evening. When morning came, he knew that would no longer be the case.

The next day, Tayyip headed to Al Taqaddum Airbase. He wore a dark blue suit with a white collared shirt and blue tie. He was clean shaven and alert, not wearing his mourning outwardly. He wouldn't give them the satisfacation.

He waited patiently in line at the check-out counter. A long silver box and a small duffle bag were his only possessions. As he casually waited for his luggage to be weighed, he looked around at the other passengers.

The attendant looked at the scale before turning to him. "Sir, your luggage is overweight."

Tayyip pulled a folded piece of paper from his wallet. The attendant unfolded the paper, looked at it, and nodded. She typed something on her keyboard. "There you are, sir. We will take your luggage. Have a nice flight."

Tayyip put the paper away and nodded. "Thank you." Nothing else needed to be said. The paper provided validity for the overweight luggage.

The rest of the trip to America was effortless. Once he landed, Tayyip made his way to the office of his old banker, Ron Stevens. "Your accounts are all frozen, Mr. Nafisi," he said.

Tayyip said, "Check again."

Ron rebutted. "This is the third time I have checked."

"Check again." Ron reluctantly reentered Tayyip's account information into the computer. Tayyip watched as the man's facial expression went from annoyance to disbelief.

"Okay, Mr. Nafisi. It looks like the account is activated again."

"Good. This is what I need." He slipped a piece of white paper to the banker. Ron looked up in disbelief as he read the writing.

"Is there some mistake?"

"No."

Ron slightly choked. "Today, sir?"

"Yes, in twenty dollar bills."

"Let me get my supervisor. I will be right back."

"Take your time," Tayyip said.

Chapter Three:
Haunting Memories

Amanda walked in the house, heading right to her mother's room. The door was closed. She opened it slowly, peering into the room. Jennifer Koppell was lying on the bed in a white silk robe. It looked as if she hadn't moved all day.

The creak of the door opening caused her to turn her head casually. "Hi honey."

"Mom, when are you getting up?"

"In a minute."

Amanda sighed, wishing her mother was...different. Then again, it wasn't all that great when she was alert. She debated going to her room or out to the living room, but, instead, she chose to set her bag down on the bed. She went to the corner of her mom's room and began playing with the pieces of a partially finished puzzle.

About an hour later, her mother looked at her, almost seeming startled she was there. "It's time, Amanda. Go get ready."

"Really?" Amanda whined.

"Yes, don't fuss about it. It's for your own good."

Within an hour, Amanda was drenched in her own sweat. She wore sweat pants, a t-shirt, and tennis shoes with her hair pulled back in a ponytail. She looked, and felt, exhausted. The large backyard looked like a paradise for small children playing war and other imaginative games. It represented something far from that for Amanda though. The yard was a wartime mock-up. Instead of grass, a majority of the yard was sand. Tents and large holes peppered the grounds. Random objects popped up from a variety of places, as if they were combatants. Jennifer held a clock, watching her daughter. She clearly wasn't happy, but she always showed respect.

Jennifer barked out. "Just ten more."

Despite her small frame, Amanda held a large medieval sword in her hand. Her shoulders and arms ached from holding it up for so long. She was exhausted from holding such an awkward weapon for a twelve year old girl. Today, her mother made her wear a glove that was irritating her skin and making her even warmer, almost to the point where she was positive she would faint.

Amanda said, "I can't swing anymore." Her arms began to droop downward, unable to support the weight of the sword any longer.

"Just ten more. Pick up your arm."

"Mom, no. No more," Amanda pleaded. Her request ignored, she showed a rare act of defiance. She dropped her sword and walked into the house, past her mother.

Jennifer stayed outside, frustrated. She walked over to the sword and picked it up. Disgusted, she threw it back down. She slumped to the ground and covered her face with her hands. It was just too much sometimes. Life was hard, she got that, but did it have to be so damn hard all the time.

Finally ready to move, Jennifer got up and walked into the house. In the kitchen, she poured a glass of water from the tap. A prescription bottle filled with pills say on the table. She opened the bottle and stared at the tablets. Dumping two of the pills into her palm, she popped them into her mouth and washed them down. Once the pills had a few moments to kick in, she made her way down the hallway to peek at Amanda, who was already asleep in her room. Jennifer stood there, staring at her little girl. She had turned into a near teenager seemingly overnight. Jennifer had been present, but she knew she'd missed a lot. The fact that she loved her daughter so much didn't escape her though. Lingering at the door, she debated whether to leave or go to the girl. Eventually she crept over and gently rubbed Amanda's head, leaning down to kiss her flushed cheek goodnight.

Jennifer went back to her room and stared at her bed. Would she ever get used to not seeing him there? It didn't seem like it. She couldn't forget. She wouldn't forget.

Her mind drifted off to thoughts of that day:

The sand had been moving forcefully, ripping into Issac Rainnek's eyes. He waited there with his hands tied behind his back. He was wearing his uniform - a t-shirt, Army pants, and his combat boots. His face was clearly distraught. Three men were lying on the ground around him. Fires were blazing everywhere, making heat waves ripple even more intensely in the hot desert air.

On the war grounds, a blow torch was near his face, instilling fear into him. Then, without warning, there was a heavy blow delivered to his back from a guerilla war soldier. Two ropes were tied around his waist and each was attached to the front grill of a Hummer. Soldiers sat in each one, looking eager. A command was given and one of the Iraqi men put the Hummer in reverse. Issac's face tensed up and he gritted his teeth, trying to endure the torturous pain. He could feel the tendons in his joints weakening from the strain, slowly ripping because they couldn't resist the opposing forces any longer.

Helicopters flew past overhead. The rescue team watched the scene unfold. They spotted the missing soldiers. Their helicopter circled the area to find a safe landing spot. Jennifer was on that rescue team. She struggled between her combat skills and the aching of her heart at seeing her husband down there, being tortured and on the cusp of death. She grit her teeth down and began to fire her gun, hoping to make direct contact with the guerillas below. They fired back, not afraid of death. They'd trained for that their entire lives.

Scattered bodies of dead US soldiers and guerillas were everywhere, littering the desert like they were flyers on the Vegas strip. Somewhere close by, a bomb exploded. Afterward, the helicopter landed on the ground and Jennifer charged out, surveying the scene further, and ready to take action.

Instead of a gun, she now had a grenade launcher. She was locked and loaded, ready to fire at the man in the Hummer, who was delightfully focused on ripping Issac's body apart. She fired, easily hitting her mark. The truck exploded. She ran toward Issac, hoping she wasn't too late to save him. He was barely alive when she ran over. She pulled a knife from her boot and started cutting him free. As she sliced through the ropes, she begged him to hold on. She believed he could make it. However, his spine had been snapped, leaving him paralyzed from the waist down. He was in so much pain that he could barely talk.

Issac said, "I'm sorry. I love you."

"Don't worry, hon. You're going to be okay."

Barely able to move without showing the horrendous suffering he was enduring, Issac shook his head no. "Please Jenny, take your knife and slit my throat."

"No! Please don't ask me to do that," Jennifer said.

"I can't take it. You have to."

He was so weak, hardly able to breathe air in. Jennifer's tears streamed down her face as she held him. She looked into his eyes and saw that they were stuck in one place. Gun shots rang out in the background as she stared down at the man she loved so much . Gently, she slid the blade of her knife across his throat. His eyes bulged at first but they quickly closed and peace overcame him.

Jennifer jumped up from her bed, feeling as if the enemies from that day were with her. She ran out her kitchen door and into her backyard, staring at it in the moonlight. Her expression was blank as she assessed everything she saw. It seemed so foreign to her, yet it was a reminder of what she'd lost, what she struggled to forget on a daily basis. Anyone else would not have made their backyard a reminder of that horrible day. She felt that if she let it go, it would dishonor Issac and all he meant to her as a soldier and more importantly, as her husband, the man she loved.

Inside, Amanda had awoken, both from her mother's footsteps and the door banging against the wall. The young girl ran into the kitchen and looked out the window. She ran into the backyard and gently called to her mother. The older woman didn't respond. Amanda walked over to Jennifer and gently shook her arm. "Mom, come back inside." Jennifer's eyes fluttered open and she moved her head around, looking confused. Amanda smiled and hugged her.

"I must have…"

"It's okay, Mom. It must be the medicine."

"Maybe," she replied.

"You should stop taking it."

Jennifer retorted. "But I need it." They walked back into the house, arm in arm, and this time Amanda tucked her mother back into bed.

Chapter Four:
The Best I Can Be

Hermosa Beach, California, January 30, 2014

Shane sat inside his 1969 Mustang at the ocean's edge, staring at the water kicking up small waves. His hand was wrapped around a brown paper bag-covered bottle, just like a bum might do on the street. He was evidence that you didn't need to be homeless to feel like a bum, like you didn't have any value left to give in life. Suddenly bored with it, he got out of the car and popped open his trunk, tossing the bottle in. It clanged against the hundred empty bottles already scattered in the trunk. That was it...his dirty little secret. He kept it hidden away in the trunk of his Mustang, hoping that nobody would know where he spent the few dollars he had left. It was better than any other damn drug they could give him for numbing the pain. Just as he was ready to slam the trunk shut again, his eyes averted to one bottle in the back corner. It was vodka. Perhaps that would do the trick to fill the void. He grabbed it and went back into the car.

A couple of girls walking on the beach looked over at Shane, wondering what his deal was. He gave her a huge smile and saluted them with his middle finger before revving up the engine, kicking up sand and exhaust as he exited the beach. He laughed as he heard them screaming, "Crazy asshole." They were right and he didn't care.

With all his windows rolled down, Shane could feel the cool wind whipping on his face, invigorating him slightly as he made his way home. It seemed to take the almost-drunken edge off. The weather in Hermosa Beach was almost always beautiful, giving a false illusion to its residents' happiness, in Shane's opinion anyway.

Shane needed to get home to make sure he was there for Emily. Her school day was almost done. As he rounded the corner into the subdivision, he pulled into the garage.

Emily's bike was already lying on the grass at the edge of the yard, not too far from the brick and stone mailbox. He opened up the box and saw a peculiar envelope inside. There was no stamp, indicating that it didn't come through the Post Office.

The cream colored envelope had a red wax seal on the back. On the front, he found a fancy deep black cursive handwriting that was most eloquent. Maybe it was an invitation to a party or something like that. He pulled it out and grabbed the handful of bills that demanded urgent attention. He sighed as he walked into the house, hiding the mail underneath a pile of other bills that had gone unopened. What was the point of opening up a bill you couldn't pay?

"Emily, you here?" He didn't hear a response so he walked to her room to see if she had her ear buds in or something. As he knocked softly, the door swung open. The room was clean, much cleaner than the rest of the house. "Emily, you in here?"

Emily jumped up from the bed and screamed. Shane moved back, acting frightened before smiling and hugging his daughter. "You got me, kiddo. How was school today?"

"We learned how to cook a frog," Emily said.

"A frog?"

"Yeah, Mrs. Mary showed us. When she opened the box the frog was still alive, saying, 'ribbet, ribbet.' It stared at us, pleading for its life," Emily said, widening her eyes and pressing her hands together as if she was praying.

"You're quite the story teller," Shane said, not allowing his mind to relive that scene again. "So, did you try it?"

"Ew, Dad."

Shane laughed with his daughter, the single bright light in his day, each and every day. She meant the world to him and he never shied away from showing everyone that. He saw a book on the bed. "What book is that?"

"It's called the Frog Jumpers."

"Is that on your reading list? I don't remember seeing it."

"Dad, it's on there."

"Hey, you know I've been looking for work during the day, but I'm going to start picking you up from school. It'll give the neighbors a break. What do you think? That way you don't have to use your key to come in the house and I don't have to wonder if you're home."

"And where were you, Daddy?"

"I was at the beach thinking about how I am going to support us," he answered honestly. Lying to his kid was something he vowed to never do. "And...I was thinking about us and our future. Come to the kitchen with me. I've got to make dinner. What do you want to eat?"

"Hot dogs," Emily said.

Before he knew it, evening had come and it was time to put Emily to bed. Then had to find a way to fill the void in his life that appeared when he was alone. He turned on the TV and started to flick through the channels.

He glanced over to the mail pile in the kitchen and decided to open up the cream envelope. "Might as well see what it is," he mumbled.

He looked at the fancy envelope again, broke the red seal, and opened the flap. He pulled out its contents and found two plane tickets to Rhode Island in it: one with his name and one with Emily's name. The letter read:

You have been hand selected to partake in a new

reality show series that will provide the opportunity for you and your daughter to bond on national television. Please join us at the conference in Rhode Island. All expenses will be covered for the two of you to visit. Complete the reality series and you will receive $2,000,000.00.

Shane threw the envelope to the side, thinking it was some hoax or scam. *Who sent an invitation to a reality series that way?* he wondered. Why would they want him? His name was poison to many people and, while he didn't really care about that for himself, when it came to Emily he cared a great deal.

Knowing that he couldn't avoid it, he decided to go to the bill pile next. It was the perfect expression of just how depressing and hopeless his financial outlook was. He didn't have money to pay the late fees, much less the bill itself. He did not have a single bill that wasn't past due. And now the mortgage holder had started the threats of foreclosure. It was so damn frustrating. Even if he found a decent job, it'd take him years to pay off all the bills he'd fallen behind on. Sick of what they reminded him of, he tossed the bills aside and his mind ventured to another nightmare – the days of war.

He dozed off, going into the dreams that he kept bottled up. He replayed the brutal murder he was part of and when he awoke, he found himself drenched in cold sweats, remembering the boy reaching out to him for help. Shane glanced at the clock. 4:45 a.m. He rubbed his face and went to the bathroom for a drink of water. When he came back to the living room, he noticed a CD-

ROM that had half fallen out of the cream envelope. He picked it up and read the label: Come Discover *The Land of Paintings*.

Bringing his laptop over, Shane loaded the CD-ROM into the player and watched it come to life. A man who introduced himself as Mathew Lengyel was sitting at a desk wearing a dark blue suit. He stared at the camera and Shane felt like he was staring right into his eyes, reading what was on his mind, and piercing his soul with his words. It was spooky, but he wouldn't turn away.

"Have you ever wanted to be a hero to someone? Have you ever wanted to make up for something you didn't do right? Here is your chance to introduce something new to the world, be a hero, and support your family at the same time. Give us an hour and we will give you a new life. Two million dollars is a lot of money, Shane. Think about it. Can you really afford to pass up hearing about this opportunity? It's time to get up off the couch and come to The Land of Paintings. We eagerly await you and your daughter, Emily."

Shane hit the eject button on the computer, wanting to get the CD-ROM with the personal message out of his computer. How the hell did that guy know what was going on in his life? The mistakes, well that wasn't confidential, but whoever Mathew Lengyel was, he was a nosy bastard – exemplifying the big brother attitude that so many people had and Shane tried to run from. He was suddenly on high alert, instincts in overdrive and feeling paranoid, like someone was watching him. He grabbed the tickets and studied them closely. They were first class and dated the next day. What was this about?

He started to search The Land of Paintings on his computer and didn't come up with anything. This was odd, especially if it was a television show. From what he understood, they promoted the heck out of new TV programs in order to gain hype and find contestants to audition. He had an invitation to be a part of a game with a huge cash prize, but no one knew it existed. It was suspicious, to say the least.

The next search that Shane did was for Mathew Lengyel, looking him up in the IMDB database. He had producer credits for some fairly popular shows on the ABC Family network so he seemed legit. He kept looking but couldn't find anything that wasn't on the up and up with the guy. Before Shane realized it, morning had come and it was time for Emily to get up. He tucked away the envelope, closed down his computer, and went to get ready for the day.

Making his way to the kitchen, Shane began to make eggs and bacon for breakfast. He thought about the letter and wondered if it was something he and Emily should at least investigate. They'd already forked out over a grand just for two first class tickets to get them there to listen. What would it hurt? They were also covering the bill just to explore it. He loved the thought of solving his money problems with $2,000,000. There was no doubt about it, that amount of money would definitely make his financial life rosier, even if the rest of his life was a battle of his internal demons against the motivation to do right by his daughter.

With breakfast on the table, Shane went to wake up Emily. "Rise and shine. Time for school," he said.

He walked back out to the kitchen and Emily joined him a few minutes later. She looked at the breakfast in front of her and said, "Dad, I wanted cereal."

"This is better for you. Don't worry about it; just eat it. How would you like to take a trip this weekend?"

"Where?" Emily asked. Her eyes widened and she clearly was not able to imagine where they'd go. Her dad didn't say anything about it very often, but she knew that they didn't have a lot of money. It didn't take words to make her understand that.

"Rhode Island," Shane said.

Emily looked at her dad curiously and broke out into a smile. "A weekend with you would be pretty awesome."

Chapter Five:
Seems Simple Enough

Jennifer sat at her kitchen table, staring at all the bills that were demanding her attention. She had no solution on how to pay money out that she didn't have. Instead, she tried to distract herself with the morning newspaper. Nothing good or exciting in there either. "Just do it," she grumbled, grabbing the pile of bills.

The first letter was regarding her home mortgage. It had delinquent scrawled across the top in bold red letters. All the subsequent letters weren't any different. Jennifer glanced at the clock. It seemed to linger at 7:59 a.m. for a very long time. Finally, it switched to 8:00. She immediately picked up the telephone, quickly dialed a number, and spoke with someone for a few minutes. After hanging up, she went over to the calendar and wrote down 3:45. That was one appointment she had to keep. Amanda could go over to Stacy's house after school.

For the remainder of the day, Jennifer gave a half-hearted attempt to look for jobs. None of them seemed like something she could realistically do. They were either lousy pay or, even worse, jobs that had hours that meant she'd never see Amanda. That wasn't an option either. She wasn't always there for her emotionally, and that was bad enough, but she still hoped for a better day and a chance to start life with a clean slate.

When 3:45 finally came, Jennifer made her way into

the building. She passed people gathered around outside discussing business, laughing, and even flirting. It made her heart ache a bit, knowing that she was in no position to move on and find happiness again, even though she knew that is what Issac would have wanted for her.

Once on the second floor of the building, she waited in the lobby for someone to take her to Claire Fauber's office. Hopefully this visit would be more beneficial than the previous ones had been. Jennifer needed answers and more importantly, she needed money – badly.

Claire was a forty-something woman who always wore the same thing: a dressy blouse, dress pants, and modest jewelry. She always had her glasses on and her hair pinned back. It was her look, when she was at work anyway.

Jennifer looked at Claire with apprehension showing in her eyes. She wanted to stay composed, but she felt like she was being scrutinized and it annoyed her. Claire was leaning back in her green leather chair, tapping her one finger upon her chin, calculating the words she was going to say carefully. It was obviously a skill that she'd mastered, knowing she worked with people who had 'delicate situations.' Unfortunately for Jennifer, knowing she was delicate made her mad, which seldom helped her get taken out of that classification.

"Look, Claire, I shouldn't have to wait for my husband's or my own money. My God, isn't it enough that we – he – gave his life for his country. They could at least help his family keep their home. I am facing foreclosure."

"I understand, Jennifer."

"No, I don't think you do," she replied to Claire. Her hands were squeezing the arms of the chair she sat in, her knuckles white from the pressure. "I have a child to take care of. This is more than just about me."

"Jennifer, I understand, really I do," Claire began. "Look, I'm not going to say there is a quick fix for you because there's not. The fact of the matter is that we are backed up and short on staff, but as soon as possible you will get your compensation."

"I have heard about this happening to other people, but I never thought I would be put in this situation."

"I know there is nothing that can take the place of your husband or the time you spent away from your daughter. I am truly sorry. I can't begin to feel your pain."

Her response was more calculated than sincere in Jennifer's opinion – something they rehearsed and were trained to say. "You can't feel my pain, or the torment of feeling like you're being left behind. I miss everything. I miss my life before the storm. Everything that meant anything to me was lost on the battlefield. My daughter is all I have to live for now." She didn't want to, but she welled up, not able to contain her emotions.

Claire sighed and finally confessed something she'd known, but hadn't dared say. "Somehow the system got you mixed up. You are reported dead on your file. I'm trying to fix it."

Jennifer asked, "What?"

"I'm sorry."

"How could that happen, Claire? It seems like someone would have to be working pretty hard to make me just disappear. As you can see, I'm here."

"The administration is at fault and I'm trying to correct it."

"That's just great – the administration. Could you be any vaguer? They obviously don't have children or know what it's like to give your life for your country," she spat. One thing soldiers hated was that the bureaucratic decisions that affected them took forever to implement, yet the bureaucrats themselves made sure their issues were handled quickly and efficiently. It wasn't about serving in those moments, it was about trusting your country to take care of you better in appreciation for the service you offered.

Claire nodded, choosing silence. She pushed a box of tissues toward Jennifer, who reluctantly took one. Eventually, she moved a blue folder closer to the former soldier. "This program can help you."

"How?"

"It will stabilize you; get you on track to a new start."

Jennifer looked at it. It was for a program for those who had problems adapting back into civilization effectively after serving or enduring a tragedy during service. "You're crazy to suggest this. They'd try to take Amanda away if I did something like this. There has to be a better way."

"What about your sister-in-law? Can she take care of her?"

"That's not fair to ask," Jennifer said, shaking and feeling like she would have collapsed if she wasn't already sitting.

"Well, this is the best I can do right now. Think about it, okay," Claire said.

Jennifer got up, delivering a half-hearted smile and left, making her way up to the 19th floor. Hopefully that appointment would go better. Heck, maybe the doctor wouldn't even be able to see her because she was supposedly dead after all.

Jennifer got off the elevator and walked over to the receptionist desk. "I need to see Dr. Chatwick please."

"Do you have an appointment?" the receptionist asked, looking at Jennifer over the top of her bi-focals.

"No, but it's an emergency."

"I recommend going to the E.R. then, ma'am."

"I'll wait," Jennifer said. The receptionist sighed, mumbling that there were no guarantees. Jennifer gave her information before sitting. A talk show was on the television, showing people bearing their souls to the viewing audience. That was something Jennifer would never do and she didn't see how people could do it. Didn't they have any sense of privacy about their problems?

"I'm glad you stopped by, Jennifer," Dr. Chatwick said, smiling as he walked into the lobby.

Yeah, right, she thought.

"Let's go back to my office." Jennifer followed him into a room. As he closed the door, he gestured for her to take a seat.

"You wanted to discuss the medication you were on. I think that's a good idea. I'd like to discontinue the Lorazepam. There is a new FDA approved drug designed specifically with the war veterans in mind that I think is worth a try."

"I don't like the sound of that any better. How can a drug target war vets?" she asked.

"Well, it targets symptoms that many have," the doctor said, unfazed by her doubts. "There is no reason to be alarmed. What I mean is that they studied the effects of war-induced illnesses to come up with a better, more effective drug with fewer side effects."

"Such as?"

"Wanting to be secluded and away from the realities of the real world."

"My side effect is sleep-walking."

The doctor handed Jennifer a small bottle which was sealed with a pop-off cap. "Make sure you throw the old one away."

"I have it. Here you go," Jennifer said, reaching into her purse and pulling out the pills that she always kept close by. Even if she couldn't take them whenever she wanted, they gave her comfort when they were nearby.

"Very well. I look forward to updates on this medicine. It'll take a few weeks to reach its full potential. Let me know how it is going after a few weeks or if you experience any side effects that you are concerned about."

"Should I make an appointment?"

"No, that's not necessary," Dr. Chatwick said. To Jennifer that basically meant: I really don't care if it's working so long as you are good enough that I don't have to figure out what's really going on.

Then the doctor was off, putting Jennifer Koppell out of his mind and moving on to his next patient.

Jennifer left, taking her time driving toward Stacy's so she could process everything that was flooding her mind. What she wouldn't give for one day of thoughts that weren't filled with torturous nightmares and a sense of hopelessness.

"Hey, how did it go?" Stacy asked the second Jennifer walked into her house.

"Okay, the doctor is giving me something new to try. Hopefully it works."

"It'll be okay," Stacy said, smiling brightly and showing that eternal spark in her bright blue eyes. Jennifer admired her greatly. She'd lost her brother, Issac, and realized her marriage was on shaky ground all at the same time. Somehow, Stacy handled it with strength and dignity, two things that Jennifer felt slipping away from her with each passing day.

"Hey Mom," Amanda said, giving Jennifer a hug.

"Hi kiddo. Ready to go?"

"Yep, I'll get my things."

As Jennifer and Amanda made their way home, they talked about school and how Jennifer's day was. Amanda asked, "Can we please skip training tonight, Mom?" I have a project for school and I'm so tired. Please!"

"Okay, we can double up this weekend," Jennifer said. She wasn't in the mood to argue and, quite honestly, she was so wiped out that she just wanted to crawl under her covers. She hoped she woke up in bed in the morning, not in the yard or somewhere else in the house, and that she had an entirely new attitude...oh, and some money in her bank account.

They pulled into the driveway and Amanda ran to get the mail. Jennifer went into the kitchen, trying to see what she could find from some basic ingredients to make as gourmet a meal as one could with two thinly sliced pork chops, which was the only meat she had.

"Hey Mom, look at this," Amanda said, running into the house. Her cheeks were flushed and she looked completely curious.

"I don't know," Jennifer said, looking at what she was holding. It was a white envelope with a red seal on it. It looked very fancy. "Maybe a wedding invitation or something. I'll open it later. Why don't you go wash your hands and get started on that homework while I cook?"

"Aw," Amanda said, turning around to do as she was told.

Jennifer grabbed the mail, cringing at the bright red letters that spelled out *URGENT,* and growled under her breath.

"Did you say something, Mom?" Amanda called out.

"No, just grumbling, hon." Jennifer called out to her daughter, amazed at how well the child's hearing was when she would rather be tuned out.

That night, Jennifer began taking her new medicine. She hoped that it would make a difference, really do what everyone hoped it would. She knew that nothing would make both her and Amanda happier. After swallowing the small red pill with a glass of water, Jennifer went over to the elaborate white envelope that had been delivered to her. She was surprised to see that there was no postmark on it. Someone had dropped it off. Interesting.

She pulled out a letter, a smaller envelope, and a CD-ROM. She read the letter first.

You have been hand-selected to partake in a new reality show series that will provide the opportunity for you; your daughter, Amanda; your sister-in-law, Stacy; and her two children, Christy and Clark, to bond on national television. Please join us at the conference in Rhode Island. All expenses will be covered for the five of you to visit. Complete the reality series and you will receive $2,000,000.

Jennifer stared at the odd note, trying to determine if she was an idiot to think it was real. It sounded too good to be true, which meant it probably was too good to be true. She opened the small envelope and pulled out five first class tickets to Rhode Island for February 1, 2014 – just two days away.

She put the CD-ROM into her computer and listened to a man, Mathew Lengyel, talk directly to her about the reality series, The Painted Catch.

"Jennifer, I know you have been longing to be the hero in your daughter's life once again, to be there for

her in a way you haven't been for quite some time. The same is true for your sister-in-law and her children too. This opportunity will provide you with the means to make up for something that went wrong. It's your chance to introduce something new to the world, be a hero, and support your family at the same time. If you all give us an hour, we will give you a new life. Two million dollars is a lot of money, Jennifer. Think about how it would save your home and allow you to send Amanda to that school she longs to be at. It's time to realize that it's not the medicine you take that will make you better; it's the actions you can take. I welcome you to come to The Land of Paintings. We eagerly await you and your family."

Jennifer picked up the telephone and called Stacy. "Hey, got a minute?"

"Is everything okay?" Stacy asked groggily. "It's midnight."

Jennifer looked at the clock. "Sorry, I lost track of time, but I have to talk to you right now."

Jennifer went on to explain what she reviewed and Stacy was suddenly wide awake. "Do you think it's legit, Jennifer?"

"I don't see the harm in seeing if it is. There's no commitment except an hour meeting."

"Well, it looks like we're making a little trip to Rhode Island. Should be fun. I've never been there before."

That night, Jennifer had no idea what her new medicine may or may not be doing because she couldn't sleep. So many questions went through her mind. She knew she had skills enough to win any reality show competition, mentally or physically. If it was a real opportunity, she wouldn't squander it...and it was legit.

Chapter Six:
Welcome to The Land of Paintings

Rhode Island, February 1, 2014

Mathew Lengyel knew how to captivate an audience to get results. His slight balding mixed with gray hair made him look older than a guy in his early 50s, but he pulled it off well, using it to his advantage. It made him look less high roller and more fatherly, more wise.

He was standing there, speaking in a modern room that somehow managed to pull off a quaint feel. There were black granite floors glossed and shined to perfection with windows that were hidden by gray blinds. A flat screen television was attached to the wall, the focal point of the entire lecture room. He looked compellingly at his audience, sharing the excitement of the opportunity. It was a rather small audience though, consisting of only two members: Shane Braff, a very athletic muscular man in his late 30s, and Emily Braff, a tall slender 10-year old with long hair. They both wore jeans, t-shirts, and tennis shoes.

"As I was saying," Mathew continued, "the advantages far outweigh the disadvantages. You will go down in history. In fact, you are making history right now. You two will be the first to experience The Land of Paintings." Emily sat there, holding her favorite doll, and watching the speaker curiously. She didn't really understand what he was saying, but she knew her daddy would and that was all that mattered.

"I thought for sure my daughter and I would not be the only ones here." Shane looked at Mathew calmly, clearly assessing what this opportunity was *really* all about. Something wasn't adding up and people, especially in the entertainment industry, didn't just easily hand over an opportunity to earn $2,000,000.

Emily asked, "Where is everyone else?"

Mathew didn't back down from Shane's gaze and abruptly burst into laughter. "Oh no, you're right, we have selected other families to partake, but we keep everyone separated."

"Why?" Emily asked.

"You will not be introduced to anyone until you either reach the finish line or complete the mission. It's part of the show's structure."

Shane still wasn't sold on what Lengyel was selling. "And we're just evaluating all the paintings?"

"Sounds simple, doesn't it?" responded Lengyel.

Emily says, "Too simple. How is that entertaining? I would turn the channel right away."

Mathew said, "You would, huh?"

Emily nodded her head yes and Shane looked over at her before commenting. "Two million dollars to look at paintings; there has to be something more to this."

"You bet there is a catch. Please follow along."

Mathew's face lit up, showing a ruddy red complexion as he peeled back some steel doors to reveal something.

Emily couldn't hide her enthusiasm. "Whoa Dad -- look!"

There were many miniature paintings enclosed in a glass wall that moved when Mathew touched a button. He slid one up and began rotating it like it was on a carousel. In one of the paintings, there was a small cabin, trees, and a full moon shining in the snowy night sky. A light shone through the window of a beautiful dollhouse within the cabin. Inside of the dollhouse, there was a family warming themselves with hot chocolate sitting around a table. Mathew saw that he had their attention now. "Surprise!"

Shane looked at him in disbelief, but he didn't care. Mathew kept on doing things that didn't seem technologically possible. He pressed a button on the hollow glass and a numeric digital code arranged itself to 2032. As the painting moved closer to the group, the frame housing it detached, folding and sliding into the casing. It was magical to watch. The oils in it started looking distended and they stretched without losing their form. Light beams trickled throughout the interlined pattern until a magnetic bubble was formed. One snowflake fell to the foreground, followed by many more. Emily's eyes dilated each time she saw a snowflake fall.

"It's beautiful," said Emily. She wasn't the only one in awe either. Shane also stared at the paintings, which were some sort of state-of-the-art design that gave them motion. A branch on one of the trees waved in the breeze, while a bunny left a trail of prints in the crisp white layer of the newly fallen snow. However, while Emily was completely entranced and enchanted, Shane was not. He was very concerned about what he saw, not completely trusting technology that was obviously top secret.

"How is this possible? It looks so real, but I know it's not."

Emily said, "Yes, I know we can't fit in there either."

"There are so many technological advances that most people in the world know nothing about. That's my job, actually. I find out about the things the government would prefer to keep under wraps. We managed to get a replica of the patent before the attorney general could do anything about it."

"And you think the government is going to just let that fly?"

"Naturally they tried to stop us, but they couldn't. Our case was solid and the attorneys that work for us were masterful."

Shane could feel his chest tighten at the word 'government,' but he tried to stay focused on the point, so she could call out BS the first chance he got.

"How do we get from painting to painting?" Shane asked.

"Good question," Mathew said, clapping his hands together. "An imaging microchip will be inserted underneath the skin of those who enter and a shrink ray will allow you to reduce enough to get into each painting. We assist you with a rope for the first one, after that you're on your own. You and Emily live there in that environment until you enter the next painting," Mathew responded.

"A chip?" Shane's instincts were on high alert.

"You're saying you have created a way to make us smaller?" Emily added. "That's not possible."

"Yes, it is, Emily," Mathew replied, looking at both of them, "but it has to be done inside there." He pointed to a plasma television screen that had been showing a slide show of The Land of Paintings. The area containing the paintings showed a magnetic field surrounded by a colored ring vibrating around its perimeter.

"How do we do that?" Shane queried.

"I have a crew that will escort you and your daughter there after you sign these papers."

"Two million is a lot of money and now I see why. Come on, Emily, let's go," said Shane.

Mathew walked over, sticking his hand out. "Please, wait a minute."

"There is nothing to wait for, Mr. Lengyel. This is

not safe for me and definitely not safe for my daughter." Shane took Emily's hand. She grabbed her book bag, along with her doll, as they walked to the door.

"You can't afford to just walk out on an opportunity like this, Mr. Braff, and you know it."

The words caused Shane to pause, turning back to look at Mathew, whose mannerisms had taken on a different tone.

Shane says, "You don't know anything about me." He, once again, turned to leave.

"I know you have a dishonorable discharge and you can't keep a job because you don't know how to cope with all the things you've been through. The only way you cope is by taking it out on the bottle. Just think how nice you'd feel if you could buy that dollhouse you have wanted to get for Emily."

"How did you know about that?"

"All you have to do is take a chance," said Mathew, ignoring Shane's question.

With slow, deliberate words, Shane tried to keep his composure with Mathew Lengyel. "No, all I have to do is walk away and find a way to do it myself. Do you think I am going to let you play with me and my daughter? God only knows what could happen with that. I can't afford to have you use us as your human guinea pigs."

"The effects only last when you are inside the area. Once out, everything is back to normal," Mathew said.

"What about all the things that can go wrong inside there?" Shane asked, pointing to the high tech world of the paintings that they'd just seen.

"You are a trained combat commander. I think you can handle it. It's part of the reason you were invited. We obviously can't have just *anyone* doing this."

Shane took another step, determined to resist a financial solution that would solve some of his problems; though certainly not all of them. "Where are you going, Shane?" Mathew called out. "You had a one way ticket. Do you have enough money to get home? The fact of the matter is, we want you, Shane, and we will do anything to get you. That's why we offered *you* the two million dollars. Your situation makes you sympathetic to the viewers." Mathew moved around to the front of the desk. "They are going to love you because you're strong. You know how to suffer and endure, but you also know how to think. You are highly intelligent and, honestly, I'm honored to be in your presence. The job is yours for the taking. One hour, two million dollars, and a new start without any further hassles from us. How bad could this show be if we are going to show it on national television during prime time? We merely want to get everyone's attention and we know you can do it."

"What about Emily?"

"That should make you loosen up a bit. We wouldn't involve a child in something that would be detrimental to either of you."

Shane said, "Look, I don't like this. Where is everyone else? Why didn't you say anything about this before you flew us out here?"

Mathew said, "I wouldn't waste your time, Mr. Braff. Just trust me."

"You want to play God, Mr. Lengyel, is that what this is about?"

Mathew put his hands into his perfectly pressed trouser pockets. "This is about you and the choices you make."

Shane's temper began flaring. The veins on his forehead popping out as he stated, in no uncertain terms, what was on his mind. "I will not play with my daughter's life for you or anyone else. I've already lost my . . ."

"Your wife, Mr. Braff."

"How long you been watching me?"

"Let's just say I know more than you think. If you agree to enter The Land of Paintings, your daughter will never have to worry about anything in her life again. Surely that means something to you."

"You don't know me," Shane said once again.

"I know you can't get your own government to pay you," Mathew said. "They guaranteed that when they gave you the dishonorable discharge, yet you did nothing dishonorable when it really gets down to it. You're a victim of politics, of PC."

"It's a computer error. It will be fixed soon."

"I'm sure that's what you hope, but let's be real. The government could correct that with the click of one box in their computer system and they haven't. It's a shame, after all you've done for your country. How long are you going to wait? What are you going to do in the meantime? Stop lying to yourself. You know that those checks are never going to make it to your mailbox. It's time to admit it."

"That's part of the reason why I'm here, which you obviously know if you've been watching me so damn close."

"For the money, Shane, that's why you're here."

"How can I really be sure of that?"

"Well, you're kind of an open book so you're not hiding anything, very well anyways. This contest will be syndicated live during the Super Bowl. You and your child will become celebrities overnight."

"Why would I want to be a celebrity? That's my first thought. Second of all, you're interrupting the Super Bowl game to show *us* inside there?"

Mathew said, "The ratings will be through the roof. It is the best attention grabber and the next family will have a regular prime-time slot on one of the network stations, like ABC or NBC. You're the lucky ones. You get in a few hours what it will take these actors the whole season to do. We're putting all the rating whoring, so to speak, on you and your daughter."

Emily had been looking back and forth between her dad and Mathew Lengyel, trying to grasp everything they both were saying. "How long will it take to complete the mission?" She had clearly gained some of the military lingo from her dad over the years, evaluating everything as clearly as if she was an adult.

"As long as you take, but we are estimating no more than one hour and our evaluations and statistics usually prove to be most accurate. Once inside the area, you have to enter the first painting within the first two minutes of your size changes or you will forfeit the game. Everything captured within that painting can and will interact with you, adjusting your story and options as you go along. Once the next painting is drawn, you can and do have the ability to move on to it. During that time, you can bring things out of one painting and into another, but you have to remember that anything can follow you from painting to painting as well. It's pretty simple," Lengyel said.

"You call that simple?" Shane spat.

Emily tugged on her dad's t-shirt and looked at him with her large pretty eyes. "Dad, don't worry about me.

There is no way he can do what he says. He has to have a fake screen or something. Whatever it is, we can beat it. Piece of cake, right?"

"They are trying to take us for idiots, Emily. I have to be smarter for you."

"The only real catch is that if you get stuck in a painting after it dries, you have to stay there until you find your own way out. There are many ways out though, but you'd have some things to deal with. You do have to fight it at your own risk."

Shane said, "Sounds like a gladiator scene."

"We give you everything you need for success," Mathew replied, smiling at Shane as if it was no big deal. Well, to him, it was.

"Let's go, Emily."

Mathew said, "If you wish."

Shane turned to Emily, who was growing more defiant. He could see that look in her eyes, it was the same one his wife had always had when she was determined. He knelt down, looking into her eyes at eye level. "Honey I don't want anything to happen to you. I love you and I couldn't stand being responsible if anything bad ever happened to you."

"Dad, I know that. We're going to be together and you'd never let anything happen to me. Besides, it's going to be aired on national television. They have censors and things like that, right?"

Shane said, "When did you get so smart?"

"You've taught me well, Daddy."

Shane sighed. He could fight Mathew Lengyel better than her. "You sure you want to do this?"

"Yes, we could really use the money, Dad."

Shane stood up and walked toward Mathew, staring him directly in the eyes. "I want the money wired to my account before I go inside," he demanded.

Mathew said, "Done. Sign here. You'll just have to sign this rescission clause in case you don't make it. It states that the bank will return the wire."

Shane shook his head, questioning his sanity. He wouldn't be the first person to do a hell of a lot for a big load of cash. He sat back down in the chairs he and Emily were in earlier, leaned forward, and browsed the contract that Mathew had slid in front of him.

Shane asked, "How can you say it's done? You don't even have my account number."

Mathew placed his hands behind him, thinking about how best to answer. "Let me show you something on the computer," he said, pulling up a transaction page.
"What is your account number?"

Shane pulled out his wallet and reached for a card in one of its folds. "Here it is."

Mathew said, "Okay, your bank is Capital One. It will be done in less than three minutes." Shane looked over at Emily, who smiled brightly as she watched everything happening.

"I need to make a phone call," said Shane.

Shane called his automated banking service and heard the robotic voice telling him his account's status: last deposit in the amount of $800. on November 20[th.] Your ending balance on January 31st is negative $4.78. He ended the call and turned to Mathew, who was typing away on his laptop.

"Are you satisfied?" Mathew asked.

"Why would a negative balance satisfy me? There is no money in my account," said Shane.

Mathew listened, tapping his fingers casually. He didn't say a word so Shane continued. "I want to know all the money is in my account like you said. I will wait here with my daughter until the transaction is cleared."

Mathew clears his throat. "Well I see..."

Shane interrupted. "You can make arrangements for me and my daughter or we can sleep here on the floor in your office." Mathew picked up the phone on his desk and pressed a button, putting it up to his ear.

Shane looked at Emily and she smiled at him. Mathew replaced the phone. "You are to stay at the Wark La' Hesten Hotel. You are to arrive back here the minute you hear the transaction has been cleared. You will have approximately fifteen minutes to get here and your every move will be watched by privately hired secret service."

"Hired by whom?" Shane asked.

Mathew said, "Myself and my colleagues. We are not the type of men to just toss out $2,000,000. I'm sure you can appreciate that."

"Who are you working with?"

"You will know, in due time."

"I don't have time to play games; especially when my child is involved."

"You are going to be a very rich man within minutes and back on your way to enjoy your life right after Sunday's game. I understand that you're worried about things going wrong. Go to the hotel, wait for clearance, come back, and have the time of your life with your daughter in this innovative amusement space. Write home about it if you want."

"Don't patronize me. If you are going to make a fool of us on national television, at least give me the respect that I deserve."

"You're okay," Lengyel mused. "There will be no calls going in or out of your room, Mr. Braff. You are allowed to check your bank, but make sure the time is right because you only get one call – that's it. You'd better be back here within 15 minutes of that call or the deal's off. Don't try anything stupid because there are always eyes on you. Two million dollars is a lot of money and you, Mr. Shane Braff, are a millionaire now. Congratulations, it's a done deal."

Shane scribbled his signature on the contracts and handed the papers back to Mathew. "Is that it, Mr. Lengyel?"

"Why don't you check your bank one more time…just to be sure," Mathew offered.

Shane did that and, this time, the news was better. A deposit of $2,000,000 had been made, leaving a positive balance of $1,999,995.22.

He hung up the phone and nodded, completely uncomfortable with what was happening, but there was no turning back.

"From your expression, I can tell that you won't need that hotel room after all. Everything is settled here. Let the cameras start rolling and let the games begin. Good luck, Mr. Braff. I'll be watching. The whole country will be watching." Mathew got up and left as two men in white coats and white jeans came into the room.

One of the men said, "Follow us."

* * * *

Mathew watched as Shane and Emily left his office and before reaching down to pick up his phone. "Send in

Ms. Koppell and her family."

Jennifer and Amanda, followed by Stacy, who was holding baby Clark, and Christy, her twelve year old daughter, walked into the room. They were greeted with a warm, enthusiastic smile.

"I'm so glad you could all join us. This is indeed an honor and I'm looking forward to sharing the exciting plans I have in store for you," Mathew said, walking to each lady and introducing himself, then smiling at the children.

Jennifer watched him, thinking he was like a politician vying for votes.

"Please, sit down. I'm sure you're eager to hear what this is all about," Mathew said.

"Yes Mr. Lengyel, I am," Jennifer said, taking the lead.

"I know you're a woman of resources and action, which is why we need you."

"What is The Painted Catch exactly?" Jennifer asked.

"Right to the point. I like that. First of all, let's just say that it is a game that requires you to use your intellect and skills to navigate through it."

Jennifer smiled. "Then why would you need my entire family and not just me?"

"For ratings purposes, of course. You see, it's going

to be broadcast to the entire country...during the Super Bowl in fact."

"That's tomorrow," Jennifer said. "Even if I agree...we agree...I didn't coordinate anything to be gone that long."

"No worries. This is not something that will require long at all. In fact, if all goes well for you, you'll be on your way home Monday morning, a considerably richer woman."

"And if it doesn't go well?" Jennifer asked. She glanced at Stacy and saw that she was also focused on Mathew for that question.

"Things couldn't be worse for you, could they?" he answered.

Jennifer frowned. Double questions with implied meaning had always irritated her, grating on her every nerve because she was a person of logic...even with all the gray areas of her life at the moment.

"Well, don't hold back," she said.

"I prefer honesty, as I can see you are a direct person, one that doesn't like to beat around the bush."

"Who else would be in this game?"

"That cannot be revealed, but rest assured, if you make it to the end, you'll encounter them."

"But only one can win?"

"Only one," Mathew said.

Stacy interrupted. "We all know that Jennifer has skills, but what type of things can the rest of us do? After all, Clark here is just a baby and the girls are very young. What about them, and me for that matter?"

"Good questions, Stacy. Every person has a skill that they can use, a quality that they can give. It's that simple."

"What's the premise?"

Mathew explained for the second time about how they'd created the reality show on paintings that people could actually enter, making Stacy's jaw drop, and Christy and Amanda feel like they were being cast in a magical movie.

"That doesn't seem feasible, Mr. Lengyel," Jennifer said, folding her arms and staring into his eyes. She was looking for some sign of what he was really up to, but she saw nothing that she could misconstrue in any way.

"As someone who was deeply involved with our government, I am sure you know more than anyone about how many things are possible that can be quite challenging to grasp at first mention."

"Good point," Jennifer said.

Then Mathew showed them the paintings and

explained the concept a bit further. It was risky, but he assured that it was safe and had been tested. A part of Jennifer wanted to resist and not take the easy path, but she was very aware that all of her recent thoughts had been about why life was so damn hard. This was easy and she should be grateful. In a last attempt to not look like she was so easily swayed, she asked one more question. "Look, let's just be direct. We play this game and we walk out of here with $2,000,000.00? That's it then; it's over and we're through?"

"Besides taxes and enjoying some celebrity status, it's over," Mathew said.

Jennifer began shaking just a bit and excused herself. She turned her back and reached into her purse, taking one of the new red pills. She scanned the room for something to drink.

"Water?" Mathew offered, handing her a full glass.

"Thank you," she said. She swallowed the pill and turned to him. "Let's review the contract."

Twenty minutes later, with Stacy already putting her skills as a paralegal to the test, Jennifer had signed the contract and they were all being escorted out of the office by two men dressed in white uniforms.

* * * *

Inside Mathew Lengyel's office, he was pleased. He'd accomplished his mission and now it was show time. He lounged in his chair briefly, watching the cameras that looked over the prep area. In two separate areas where they would be kept from seeing each other until the time was right, he watched Shane Braff and Emily prepare for their reality show and in another area, separated by a thick concrete wall, Jennifer and her family were preparing. It would take a full day of prep to ensure everything was right, the trackers were on, etc. It would go quickly though and then it would be show time.

Mathew was pleased. He'd successfully accomplished what he was hired to do. He couldn't say he understood it, but it didn't much matter. Business was business sometimes, no need to ask too many questions.

Reaching into his desk drawer, Mathew pulled out a cigar, which he was eager to savor – a $420 Cuban beauty that was sure to be mellow, refined, and smooth – a perfect accompaniment to the glass of 50 year old scotch Regal he was going to have with it.

He puffed in, lighting the cigar up, and waited for a messenger to arrive with a little package for him.

The messenger came precisely fifteen minutes later, showing their punctuality, and Mathew reached for the silver briefcase, thanking the man with a gracious $100 tip.

He clicked open the case and salivated over its contents. Stacks of crisp fresh hundred dollar bills were bundled into $10,000 packs. They represented him obtaining freedom and the ability to do anything he wanted for the rest of his life.

Smiling, he pressed the speaker button on his phone before pressing in the number he wished to dial, balancing the cigar in his hand as he did so.

It took only one ring for the call to be answered. Mathew said, "Thank you for my payment; it is a pleasure doing business with you." Then he hung up the phone.

Standing up and closing the briefcase, he briefly rubbed the top of it like it was good luck to do so. Then he fixed his suit, put on a different tie, and headed home, eager to see his wife and family and enjoy the weekend with them. The finale would definitely be the halftime show at the Super Bowl. It promised to be quite an entertaining halftime show.

Chapter Seven:
Counting Down

The time to start their adventure had come. Following the men in the white suits, Shane and Emily made their way down the hallway. Nobody said a word. Shane and Emily stared straight ahead, not looking at each other, but observing everything around them. So much was happening and they were trying to absorb it all. Everything was fast paced and the people running around showed that they were in the middle of a major production, a collaborative effort of many people to make it happen.

They were secured in the room and the two men in white suits that had escorted them down the hall into the corridor they were now in were all business, lacking in even more social skills than Shane did.

"Please prepare to be searched. It will take approximately 54 minutes, counting down starting now. A clock on the wall began a countdown."

"Searched? What type of search?" Shane asked.

"Basics sir. We just need to take inventory of what's on your being and make sure you don't bring any of your personal affects into the show."

"Not even my doll?" Emily asked, hugging it tightly.

"No ma'am," the one said, extending his hand out to take the doll from Emily.

She frowned at him and then kissed her doll on the head, whispering, "I'll be back soon."

Shane smiled, sensing that Emily was getting nervous now. He couldn't blame her either. His stomach was feeling restless and uneasy, not sure what to make of all this. It still seemed too effortless, but dwelling on that wouldn't change anything.

Emily breathed in deeply, squeezing her daddy's hand. The two watched as all their belongings they had with them were rolled into a scanning machine. Then they were led out into a walk-way.

Shane looked at Emily, worried for her. "You look scared."

She smiled, but it was no longer as energetic as it had been. She took something out of her pocket and threw it. It startled the men and they looked at her, wondering what was happening. "Piece of lint," she said, looking back at them.

Conversation and instructions were not a part of the plan that was unfolding after the security check. It made for a very quiet, somewhat somber, ambiance. Shane and Emily continued to look around at everything, soaking in the details, until they reached a long hallway. A large screen television was on the wall, broadcasting the pre-game show for the Super Bowl. They glanced at it as they walked down the hallway, taking another corridor behind a coded entryway.

Shane leaned in to Emily and asked, "What would your mom say?"

Emily said, "She'd say she was proud of you." Emily suddenly mastered any fears she may have had and a determined look took over as she made her way to the next place. She had no idea what was about to happen after entering The Land of Paintings, but she wasn't going to look like a wimp as she confronted it.

Now further down the corridor, the doors that led to a huge open area were buzzing as people ran around.

The two men in white turned, saying, "This is where you get off. Once inside, you will wait until it's time to enter into the painting. There will be a voice guiding you on the grounds of the first painting you enter, helping acquaint you with everything."

"How long will the voice be there?" Shane asked.

"No more than five minutes," the man replied. Then he turned to walk away, crossing his fingers in front of him as he left.

"Well, that is some rapid fire training for this," Shane said.

"Must be their standard operating procedure, Daddy," Emily said, making him laugh.

The two sat down on a couch and waited. People ran by them, nodding at them, but not acknowledging them. One man, wearing a headset and carrying a tablet, sliding between various lists and information, paused in front of them, talking with another man.

"The first painting for Braff will be The Fruitful Bliss."

"And how about..." the other man said. The man nudged his arm and put his finger to his lip, signaling for him to be quiet. He nodded his head toward Shane, who was watching and listening very closely. He wondered why it mattered if he heard the name of who he'd be competing against at that point. Would it really make a difference? It wasn't like he knew them, after all.

"Did you hear that, Dad? The Fruitful Bliss doesn't sound too bad, does it?" She smiled and patted her dad's knee before taking her small hand and looping it through his, squeezing it tightly.

"No, not bad. Now you remember to stick close by me the entire time and follow my lead for whatever comes our way. Got it?"

"Yes, Commander," she said, giggling and saluting her dad.

"That's my kiddo," he said.

Shane looked around and made sure nobody was watching him. He snuck down into his boot and pulled something out. "I've been carrying this with me for a long time. I think it's time I gave it to you, Emily."

"What is it?" she asked, eyes wide with curiosity.

"It was your mother's," he said. He held up a necklace and dangled it in front of Emily.

"Dad, it's beautiful."

"I picked a special day to give it to her. I took her out to dinner and that's when she surprised me. She told me she was pregnant with you. So you see, it was a more special day than I would have ever bargained for."

Emily smiled brightly. "Thank you so much, Daddy." She hugged him tightly, making his usually tough eyes slightly glisten. Then she put it on and felt it with her hand, smiling so sweetly and her eyes were also glistening.

"Now, whenever you need her, take that out, and you will instantly be reminded of her."

"Okay, Daddy," Emily said. Then someone came over to them and motioned for the two to follow them. They entered into a new area and Shane caught a brief glimpse through a door that was closing. He shook his head, thinking he was hallucinating. He could have sworn he saw Jennifer Koppell. *That's impossible,* he thought. *Your mind is playing tricks on you.*

"I guess this is it," Emily said.

"Let's get this done and over with as soon as possible. We're a team, right?" Shane felt compelled to hug her tightly, feeling something he didn't quite understand in his gut.

"Right, Daddy." The two separated and bumped knuckles and winked at each other – their little ritual that they'd done ever since Emily was a small child.

* * * *

"This is so wild," Stacy said, looking around. She could hardly believe everything she saw. "I've always wondered what it was like on a set."

"Hectic, to say the least," Jennifer said. She turned and looked at her sister-in-law, her best friend, and said, "Thanks for doing this. I hope it all works out. It still seems so crazy to me."

"Maybe that's what you need, Jennifer. To shake things up a bit and experience something different…it'll help you get over Issac's death and move on, which is what…"

Jennifer finished the sentence. "He'd want me to do. Yeah, I know, but all that aside, this is fucking insane."

"Mom!" Amanda frowned at her mother for swearing. Jennifer usually tried not to swear in front of her, but sometimes it just slipped out. "You owe me a quarter."

"By the time this is done, I may owe you a thousand quarters," Jennifer said.

"Good thing we're going to win and get all that money. I may bump those quarters to dollar bills…interest and all."

Jennifer laughed. "Well, I guess we just wait. We passed clearance so that's good. I'm glad we can take our things with us. Having them with me will just make me feel better," she said.

"I think they're the ones that would regret it if I wasn't allowed to have Clark's diaper bag," Stacy said, laughing at her own joke.

"So, we go into this painting and live life like normal. That sounds more like a horror show in my case than a reality show. Pretty boring too, but I guess there's a market for the bizarre and we fit the bill for what they're looking for." Jennifer looked around, staring at everything around her and doing recon, a habit that had never left her since her days of service.

A door was closing up ahead and she stared at it, hoping to get a glimpse of what was on the other side. She saw a tall buff guy with a silhouette that was definitely familiar. It reminded her of Shane Braff, which was crazy. It made her edgy because he and Dan Markel were the only ones left who could physically remind her of all the crap from her past and the anguish of the horrible decisions that he was also a part of that one day. Everyone else had passed on.

Chapter Eight:
And Your Sponsor Is

"I'm ready for my close up." A rush of activity began upon the command of one man, overwhelming everyone in the room. His voice was quiet, but his presence was huge. He sat poised, ready for the cameras to roll and begin filming. Everyone was rushing, not daring to go slow.

"Yes, Mr. Nafisi," one assistant said, pointing to everyone and barking out orders.

"We will be interrupting the network in four minutes tops," the director, Phillip, said. His shaggy gray hair was bulging out from underneath the worn out LA Dodgers baseball cap he was sporting.

"Getting the screens up. In three, two..." Phillip said.

The cameraman growled. "Get the microphone up; it's in the camera."

Phil shouted. "Quiet on the set, and three...two...one." Then he pointed to Tayyip, waving his finger downward, signaling it was show time.

A prerecorded voice fills the studio. "Your service has been interrupted to bring you a live broadcasting." The cameraman panned in, focusing on Tayyip, who was sitting in a tall back brown leather chair with a small end table next to him that had a glass of water in a crystal tumbler on it.

The click of a beam of light flipping on echoed. After that, the only thing that could be heard were the silky tones of Tayyip's voice as he spoke into the camera. He stared into it calmly, showing no anticipation, but nerves of steel and purpose.

"I am Tayyip Nafisi. I was falsely accused of a heinous crime and my family suffered dearly from the renegade actions of four US soldiers as a result. My son died due to a blow to his chest. They watched him struggle to breathe, not caring that he had asthma and had done nothing wrong to deserve such a fate.

I went to prison without any explanation as to why I was there or ability to prove that I was innocent of any wrong doing of any sort. It took the US government far too long to admit that they'd taken the wrong person and while they tried to do damage control, the damage had already been done.

I returned home to a wife who was shattered, just a shell of her former self walking this earth. I was home for no more than two days when she died by her own hand, unable to endure the pain that she'd lived through. I lost everything I ever loved just like that."

Tayyip snapped his fingers, representative of how quickly everything had been stolen from him. He leaned forward slightly, staring into the camera, exposing the audience to the pain of his soul.

"Yes, I'm angry and when I'm angry, I think. I want to show you just how greedy, selfish, and arrogant you Americans are. I am going to show you now. None of you can pass up money over goodwill. You think procedure is protocol. Just follow all the rules, no matter what. You are trained to believe that whatever you're doing is okay just as long as someone above you gives you the okay."

Tayyip went on to recall his days in prison at Guantanamo Bay, describing it in great detail from the layout of the rooms to the way he was treated. All men there had to have both hands on their knees, a chain falling from their wrists and a chain that kept them hooked to their beds. Brown sacks enveloped their faces, making it so they couldn't see anyone and two silver strips of duct tape covered their mouths when it wasn't meal time.

His voice spoke calmly and with such intensity as he described the situation. He'd rehearsed this moment a thousand times in his mind. Today was the day it went from well orchestrated plan to reality. Tayyip described scenes with the interrogators, which he called lions on the hunt.

"Do you drink water, they would ask. Yes, I would answer, trying to breath in the dense and stifling air.

The smell of blood-soaked humidity and sweat burnt my eyes daily. No time was worse than when I'd be interrogated about things that I had nothing to do with, had no part of. They didn't care and they didn't listen. Yet, I couldn't break down and speak a lie just for a reprieve. I knew I had to be more resilient than that. I could see what they were. Those men and women were dogs on a leash, yielding to the Democracy they believed they should serve blindly. No regards for life or sense of humanity running through them. They may have been made of flesh and bones, but they were robots."

Tayyip explained how all he could think of was his son and wife, the true victims in everything that unfolded that day. He'd occasionally pause and stare into that camera solemnly with his dark, expressive, brown eyes, showing the audience of the Super Bowl his soul, revealing the pain that had driven him to do something about what had been taken from him, to avenge those who harmed his family and stole his honor.

"The interrogators would ask me if I'd ever met Osama Bin Laden, if I fought in the Taliban, and if I knew of Al-Qaeda. What my answer was did not matter because they'd condemned me and wished to punish me. They were full of hate and deaf to the words of truth I spoke.

Every time I spoke the truth they'd deem it as "undesirable' and send a temperature blast through the room that would either create heat so intense I thought I would go mad, as if I was in the desert during the midday sun. At other times, there was air so cold that it was like the arctic winds howling in the night, making my fingers feel as if they would fall off. Yet, their tactics didn't work because I was driven to survive by stating the truth, knowing that I could endure what I must.

They got me confused with a man named Taan Latif, a man who knew of weapons that could do powerful and evil damage. How they got me confused with being Taan Latif alarmed me then, just as it does now. I knew they were trying to be rid of me, but I did not know why. No trial...no justice that you American's pride yourself on...nothing except for being treated horribly, like an animal. I was innocent and no one cared."

Tayyip finished his compelling speech, which came out as brilliantly as it had when he'd played it out in his mind, but the words were full of torment, despite being masterful. He looked at the camera man, who pointed and signaled that the mic was off.

He breathed in, feeling that his words had done exactly what he wanted them to.

The director looked around and called out, "Change to camera one now."

The mic was on again and Tayyip continued talking to the world from a different angle, his eyes burning with emotion.

> *"Guantanamo Bay. A place that has hooks on the floor that connect to your leg shackles and you only get to move every five hours to go to the restroom. If you have to go during that time it is too bad. You defecate right there. I was tortured and humiliated while American soldiers smiled and laughed, embracing it as if it were a comedy. That is why I am here today. I am going to return the favor and introduce to you the ultimate hoax in US history. Enjoy the show."*

The director nodded and called out for the number four camera to prepare.

* * * *

The cramped room was full of the necessary personnel as a group of people crowded into the green room, the dim light of afternoon streaming through its windows. There was a large banner on the back wall that read: *Finalists for Live Reality Show.* There were two rows with twenty chairs in each. Sitting in them were American men and women of all races and ages, waving to the cameras and enjoying their brush with possible infamy. They had not heard the words that Tayyip had said, but as he stared at them his lip raised, not believing they would have felt any remorse for what they allowed their country's supposed leaders to do.

"Mr. Jonathan Daniels, Regina Kariten, Chris Teler, and Micheal Carter," a voice called out over a speaker from behind the production booth.

All the people on the list stood up and Jonathan Daniels said, "Yes, that's me."

"Follow me please." An announcer waved his hand, telling them to come forward.

Some people move up to fill their seats, wishing to be closer. Everyone keeps waving for the camera and smiling, delighted with what they are doing. Regina motions with her mouth, "Hi Mom." Another gave a thumb up to everyone out in TV land and the last one gave a shout out to the University of Texas, giving the Longhorn symbol with his hand.

Clearly, everyone was excited for their fifteen minutes of fame on the night that had the largest viewer ratings of any the entire year through.

"And spilt screen with camera number one," the camera man orders.

Tayyip's face filled half of the screen this time and he spoke to everyone, letting them know exactly what was going on. "This is a live reality show, designed by me, Tayyip Nafisi. I am going to use you, the American people, as my deadly weapon. Stay tuned. I promise that you will be enlightened."

* * * *

The network control center was abuzz, trying to figure out what was going on and how to get back to the biggest ratings show of the year – the Super Bowl.

Coordinator: "What the hell is happening here? Get our program back on that screen now! We can't afford this kind of shit right now, no make-goods; remember the meeting."

Worker One: "Sir, I'm trying somehow; someone has gotten into our system. They're using our signal, but this message in showing on all the stations, sir."

Coordinator: "Fix it now! We are more than a quarter away from our goal of making our quota this year."

Worker Two: "They have somehow blocked all activity from inside this building. They have connected the private code on the main system and changed all access codes so no one can get in. It will be hours before anyone can even crack the code that supports their firewall to even begin dismantling or eliminating their strength signal."

Coordinator: "What and who is doing this?"

Worker One: "This is a terrorist attack, sir."

Coordinator: "Holy shit!"

Worker One: "I'll make some calls now."

Coordinator: "No! I want to figure this out. I'm not messing up our hard work buy involving anyone if we can fix it ourselves. We try first…got it? Plus, you don't know that for sure."

Worker One: "Got it sir."

* * * *

The room which Tayyip Nafisi had moved to was decorated with dark, masculine, presidential furniture. There were several flags hanging around the room behind the furniture, but the focal point was the man who sat behind the desk; an erect and composed Tayyip Nafisi.

He looked like a top official; ranked by appearance and demeanor alone. His confidence was convincing and certainly unwavering. The bright lights on his face empowered him. He looked every bit the world leader as the best known heads of state did.

Tayyip began speaking from his new location. "This war took my rights away. If anything, I was American." He paused, allowing the impact of his words to sink in. "I was proud of my adopted country, but I was mistaken for a terrorist and that is why I have this mission to accomplish. This game is...shall we say...my way of getting therapy."

Another poignant pause for the people to absorb his words and then Tayyip continued. "I don't want your sympathy. Just feel bad for the ones connected to the *infiltrators* of my journey. As you can see, I am the victim in this. I refuse to let them get away with this. Please enjoy."

The director called out that it was time to switch to

camera two and Tayyip's voice carried over while the camera exposed a new scene that was unfolding at a different location. "I am a chemist," he began. "I specialize in taking kinetic energy to a more advanced stage. Coupled with a powerful shrink ray, you have a weapon of mass destruction. I just want to have a little fun with my findings and your government's findings. You'll get to see that in action today. I was in Iraq working on a top secret mission and I wanted to share with you what your own country has been up to. What better people to use these weapons on than the people they were designed to protect. A delightful twist of irony, if I do say so myself."

He leaned closer, his dark eyes filling the screen as the camera switched back to him. "I have done numerous studies and have created my own specially designed playing field where my vision outsmarts all others. That is, my friends, a way for man to minimize in size and keep the same level of thinking as they have at their regular size. Of course, it is done while wearing a specially designed suit. Each one of my contestants will enter the paintings of my choice and fight to stay alive; think of it like a Navy Seal training camp designed by me, Tayyip Nafisi."

He breathed in, took a sip of water, and then continued to explain the rules of engagement for his game. "This is what one contestant will face. Whatever comes their way, they will have to maneuver about by their own wits and merits. As long as they have the suits on, they will be allowed to jump from painting to painting – the only catch is that they don't know what awaits them in these paintings and whatever actions they choose cause a domino effect. This place of fantasy lets them decide if they live or die. See, I'm not a cruel person by nature, but the cruel things that occurred in my life have made me rethink being good."

"There is another series of paintings, one designed to convey virtual realities, making every detail seem as if it was where you'd always been, but there will be subtle differences there that will test every survival instinct of the contestants in that painted virtual world. I think you'll find both intriguing and realistic enough that you may wonder if you, yourself, are not in such an environment. Yes, it's a true feast for the imagination and the mind. You American's tend to enjoy that type of indulgence and I certainly kept that in mind as I created every detail."

Meanwhile, Shane and Emily were being fastened into the harnesses to be lowered into their painting. Jennifer and her family were about to walk through a door into a world that they had no idea what was at that moment.

All the contestants waited and a voice sounded out over a loud speaker. "The time has come! Remember, you only have five minutes to get into your world and get started. After that, things will start to happen and you best hope you're prepared." Tayyip said the words with great joy and when he was done, his mic was turned off again and he smiled, looking at the cameras as they focused in on two very disoriented and startled looking groups of people. It was too bad that children had to be involved, but what could be done. After all, that was a part of life and Tayyip knew that all too well.

Chapter Nine:
Entering Bliss

A small drone flew by overhead, trailing a banner that read: Welcome to Your Fantasy. Then it discharged something in the air that was white and granular, kind of like sugar. The mysterious chemical landed all over Shane and Emily like contaminated rain drops and disintegrated into their suits and skin.

"It's sticky like a pesticide or..." Emily started to say, but burst out into deep coughs.

Shane would only allow for his logic to take over. "Don't buy into it, Em. They can't play God."

"Look," Emily said, pointing.

Shane looked and saw a painting that was suspended in the air. He had never seen anything like it before and it was clearly an optical illusion of some sort, something meant to distract him from what was really happening around him. There was no sign that anything was holding that painting up, not even a frame, and every color lined the ground they walked on, splattering it with rays.

"Well, we've got to get climbing. Only four minutes left," Shane said.

"You've done your surveillance," Emily said, smiling at her Dad. He knew she was teasing, but could also tell that she really did hope he had. The situation was one that couldn't be compared to anything else. "We just lower ourselves into it?" Emily asked then.

"I guess so. For such an elaborate show, they really didn't invest much time in explaining or training."

"You're the smartest guy I know. You'll figure it out," Emily said.

The two talked casually as they lowered themselves into the painting, trying to stay calm. It was strange because when they went through the portrait they truly didn't realize that they'd shrunken in size. It seemed more like the painting got larger, which was a preferable thought to Shane.

They landed on the ground and Shane was thankful to feel the grass beneath his boots. He looked at Emily, who'd already slid out of her harness and was running through the field, finding it quite enchanting.

Suddenly, a tiger roared, the sound echoing across the field. Emily screeched, running back to Shane's side.

"Was that what I think it was?"

"Did you think it sounded like a tiger?" Shane asked. Emily nodded her head yes. "Me too, but there's no way they could get a tiger into this environment."

"Seriously, Dad? Look at what they've been able to do. I didn't think they could shrink us down…can't feel a thing."

"Good point, Em. Now, let's get going."

The two began to walk and the sounds of a tiger could still be heard, despite not being able to see one anywhere. They made their way across the wheat field toward some hills in the distance, not sure what to look for or what they may find.

"Look," Shane whispered, pointing to some wheat that was swaying in a different direction from the rest of the field. The two froze and stared at the wheat, trying to assess what it was. A glimpse of orange and black flickered between the shafts of wheat and Shane put his hand in front of Emily. "It's the tiger."

"What do we do?"

"We've got to think here. Just running won't do much for us without a place where we can get a barrier between us and that thing."

Emily looked around and shook her head. "I didn't notice it before, but there's a white horse over there. Would that help? Can a horse outrun a tiger?"

"I don't know, but if my eyes are seeing the right thing, the horse has wings, which means we just might have a chance," Shane said. His heart was racing and he could feel that familiar surge of adrenaline that came when it was time for him to take action and not hesitate – accomplish the task at hand.

As they moved closer to the horse they could tell it sensed a predator. Was it them or the tiger? They didn't know, but it became clearly agitated and anxious, kicking its hooves back and high stepping, almost acting like it was trying to stop itself from stepping on a snake in the grass.

The entire time they walked slowly and Shane kept his eyes on the tiger, knowing that it could easily disappear if he lost track of it for a second. He wanted to know where that thing was at all times.

As for Emily, she was captivated by the horse, wanting to get to it as quickly as possible. "Don't you think we should just run, Daddy?"

"No, it's hard to be patient, Em, but you've got to be. Slow and easy. Slow and easy."

Shane noticed movement from his peripheral to the other side and quickly glanced. There was a woman there. "Do you see that woman, Em?"

"Yes, when did she get over there, I wonder."

"I don't know, but she's definitely there for a reason."

"She's not afraid of the tiger. Maybe its friendly, doesn't eat humans in this world," Emily offered.

"Should we go over by her?" Shane asked.

"Oh no, not yet, Daddy. I want to pet that horse. It's so beautiful."

Shane nodded his head. He couldn't blame Emily for not wanting to go near the woman quite yet. She was an eerie sight, wearing a white veil that covered her face, almost mystifying her, but still revealing the old flaky alligator skin upon her body that was weathered by the sun and looked like actual leather too. In reality, no one should have been tortured to make her acquaintance, especially with the veil covering her face. However, the sheer fabric revealed her eyes, which were very haunting. She sat there on an old, rickety, wooden rocking chair in the sun with a small table and an empty chair to the side of her.

The sun was shining down intensely, drying out the old woman's skin more by the second. In fact, the heat was getting stifling, showing that this painting, what had it been called…The Fruitful Bliss…was a rather sweltering place. Shane had no idea how he knew it so clearly, but he could tell that the chair by the old woman was for him. He'd have to get there eventually, whether he liked it or not. The thought that he was hesitant to go visit an old woman didn't escape him. He'd stared terrorists and real bad asses in the eye, but the old woman had him second guessing and calculating his every thought and move.

They kept walking toward the horse in the distance, but didn't seem to get any closer. It was as if they were walking on a treadmill and staring at an IMAX or a life size moving picture of sorts.

"It seems that everything Mathew said was right. The painting is real, Em; like any other day at the park. The air, the wind that blows. Even the sun shining above."

Emily said, "This is genius."

"He is manipulating space some way. I just don't know how. Way over my level."

"He's manipulating time and space," Emily added. Suddenly the tiger was next to them, but it only stared at them with a smile of sorts upon its face, revealing its huge incisors that could have easily shredded their flesh in a single bite.

"See, it means us no harm." Emily repeated her thought from earlier. She didn't hesitate to grab her dad's hand though, just wanting to feel his strength.

Shane said, "It's his world and we have been dropped in like solders on unsure terrain."

"I think he has this whole thing pre-recorded," Emily said. "That's the only thing that makes sense."

"What?" Shane asked.

Emily turned to her dad and smiled, shaking her head, like he was silly not to understand. "All of this we are in. I think it's pre-recorded like a tape. It's programmed to react to what they think we are going to do."

"That's pretty heavy, kiddo. It's something we don't have much time to second guess about. Let's just make sure we follow all the rules. Are you afraid?"

Emily said, "I'm just waiting for the catch, Dad." Then something caught her attention. "Look!"

"I see her," Shane said. *This is one crazy painting*, he thought.

Chapter Ten:
Back to El Paso

Jennifer stared around her, completely confused. They'd walked through a door, the five of them, and found themselves standing on the El Paso street where she lived, right in front of her home.

"Did I miss something?" Jennifer asked.

"I don't know, but I don't get it. That's for certain," Stacy said. "What is going on and why would they offer you a reward to go and live the life you'd been living?"

"Well, it makes it a bit more challenging to earn the money, I guess. Life was feeling pretty hard," Jennifer replied, feeling snarky.

"I might as well go into the house," Amanda said. "No point in standing on the street. Let's see if there's a clue or something in there."

"Okay, let me go first," Jennifer said instinctively.

"Not ready to have me test my skills yet?"

"No, not yet. Honestly, I feel like this is a dream," Jennifer replied.

"One we're all having then," Stacy said. "My car is even in the driveway, just like I left it before our flight to Rhode Island."

"Mom, does that mean that Dad's here?" Christy

asked.

"I don't know. He's busy working, I guess. I don't know why that would change."

"Do you think you two will ever be happy again?" Christy asked hopefully.

Stacy smiled at her daughter, knowing she had tried not to be bitter about her failure of a marriage, which had been quite the battle over the past years, but some of it must have shown through on occasion. Just like any kids whose world is toppled upside down, it had taken its toll on her at times, seeing Stacy cry or just feel so lonely, unsure of what came next.

"Christy, I don't think that's going to happen."

"Sorry Mom, I didn't mean to make you feel bad."

"It's okay. There would be an awful lot for the two of us to work out."

"Hey, hurry up," Jennifer yelled from her front door. She paused, staring at a yellow piece of paper on it and looked at it closely. It was a notice of foreclosure from the sheriff's office. It made her feel sick to her stomach, but she was determined to do whatever she had to in the madness of the situation.

She walked into her house and looked around. Everything looked as she'd left it – exactly – and that was freaky. The only thing different was the envelope on the kitchen table. It was the same fancy cream envelope with a red seal on it that she had received in her mailbox when she'd gotten the invitation.

"Here's an envelope. It must have instructions or something," Jennifer called out.

Everyone gathered around and watched her open it. She read the note inside it aloud:

> *"I have lined up a job for you with the Alien Species Wildlife Center. The job is available now. That is what counts and that is the only option. As soon as something else comes up you will be moved. I know it's not the best, but the pay is good, more than good. It's been almost a year since your discharge. You need to have something to occupy your time or the medicine won't work as well as it should. Hopefully you'll trust my judgment and work more effectively toward recovery."*

"Who is it signed by?" Stacy asked.

"Claire Fauber, my vet liaison," Jennifer said.

"A job though. That's a good thing," Stacy said, patting her back while she held Clark.

"Yes, but I don't get it. We are supposedly in some reality game, but here we all are, back in the lives we had and trying to figure out what the game is."

"What's more reality than the life you really live?"

"Well, I don't mind admitting, there were plenty

things from my reality that I was eager to forget about for a day…and a few million dollars."

"This is good, Mom. Do I still have to go to school?"

"From what I understood, we just had to make it through tonight," Jennifer replied.

"Aw," Amanda said.

"Well, we should get going to our house then."

"Want me to come and check it out first?" Jennifer offered.

"No, Issac taught his little sis a thing or two. I'll be fine."

"Call me when you get home, okay?"

"Got it. Love ya'."

"Love you, too," Jennifer said.

Everyone left and Jennifer sat there on her couch, not able to say a word, and trying to discern between her real life reality and the reality of the show she'd supposedly just signed on. There had to be some sign that something was different…something to differentiate between the place she'd left behind when she went to Rhode Island and the place she had entered into from Rhode Island, which looked identical to the El Paso she'd left. Boy, if she hadn't thought she was losing it before, this was sure to do the trick. She went to her purse, searching for her medicine, and popped a red pill into her mouth.

Jennifer showered and took out some clothes to wear to work the next day. She was kind of excited to be using some of her knowledge for good use, utilizing her biology and environmental degrees. Finally, sick of her own swirling thoughts about everything, Jennifer reprimanded herself for not being appreciative, and settled down to sleep. She was exhausted from the day.

Chapter Eleven:
Command Central

The television station was frantic, every worker running around and trying to figure out who'd tapped into their signal and taken their airwaves hostage – during the biggest ratings day of the year nonetheless. All the shouting of commands and snappiness from the frustration of not understanding were taking their toll on everyone, especially the coordinator, who took it personally, knowing that it was his ass on the line, regardless if he was to blame or not.

Coordinator: "This can't be happening. I can't believe it. This is going to kill us. Find out how to fix this now!"

Worker 1: "Actually sir, our exposure and ratings for the moment are at their highest – ever."

Coordinator: "What? I can't believe that. It doesn't make any damn sense. It's Super Bowl Sunday. Do you know how many diehard fans are wondering what the hell is going on?"

In the distance you could hear the telephones ringing off the hook, grating on every nerve of the coordinator who was clueless about what to do. His twenty plus years in broadcasting didn't give him any ideas, much less leads, as to how he could stop what was happening from continuing on.

Worker 1: "I understand that people were watching the game, sir. However, whoever did this knows what they're doing. The codes are all locked so no one can change the station. It's brilliant. It's also definitely an expensive attempt. You can't pull something like this off without a lot of money and some people working for you from within."

Coordinator: "Do you think it's an inside job? Someone from here?"

Worker 1: "I don't know. It seems a bit more complex than anything we could do at our level. None of us have access to everything across the board, sir."

Coordinator: "Including me. Let me see all the information you've got. I've got to try and figure something out...at least come up with a reasonable explanation for when heads start to roll, which seems inevitable."

The coordinator ran his fingers through his already balding head and you could see the perspiration stains on his pits. He was so stressed out that his cheeks were ruddy with a crimson glow, making it look like he'd just woken up from one rough night. Everyone else was silent, moving between watching him and trying to determine what had happened.

Knocking on the door, the receptionist walked into the room. She looked nervous and anxious, but she spoke up with a quake in her voice. "The FBI is here to see you, sir."

Coordinator: "Me? Why?"

Receptionist: "About the situation."

Coordinator: "Okay. This entire damn situation is getting out of control. Send them to my office and don't disturb me. Got it?"

The receptionist nodded her head and left the room. The coordinator walked away, storming out of the station's broadcast room and into his office. He didn't bother hiding the fact that he did not want to talk to the FBI and deep down, he wasn't about to admit to them that he had no clue what was happening or why. He had no control of the situation. Sure, he'd dealt with them in the past on various issues concerning the FBC, but never had he had to discuss something that people were already tossing around as a terrorist attack.

The coordinator went into his office and sat down, breathing in and trying to maintain his composure. He could feel the sweat dripping off his pits down the side of his torso, reminding him that he definitely needed to shed a good twenty pounds. The stress of the situation he found himself in may just be enough to make him do it. He literally felt sick to his stomach. He picked up the phone and told the receptionist to send the men back and then waited by his office door for them.

Coordinator: "What can I help you with today?"

Lead FBI agent: "I'm sure you have an idea. I need to see footage of all the people coming into this building for the past week." He, along with his colleagues, were all wearing black jackets with FBI written in yellow across the backs of them. You could see the outline of bullet proof vests under their clothes.

Coordinator: "Why?"

Lead FBI agent: "Seriously? Surely you have figured out that some crazy terrorist has taken over the network and we need to figure out who it is—fast."

Clearly it was not the time to play coy or make them work to get to what they wanted. Might as well confess the problem and get on with finding the solution.

Coordinator: "I cannot get into that footage even if I wanted to. It's jammed."

The men stared at him, not saying a word. Their arms were folded and they looked like they'd wait all day for him to come up with another idea before speaking again. Their intimidation by means of being patient worked.

Coordinator: "I do, however, have all the files backed up on my computer." He typed and smiled, saying, "See!"

Lead FBI agent: "Set up in here everyone."

The agent proceeded to grab his walkie-talkie and bark out some orders for everyone to prepare for setting up a command center – right in the coordinator's office. The coordinator looked at him incredulously, thinking it was nervy to just assume he could do it without even asking.

Coordinator: "Wait? Don't you need some sort of court order to do that?"

Lead FBI agent: "Not when it comes to national security. Your full cooperation *is* expected."

The agent leaned over the coordinator, showing his height and fearless nature.

Lead FBI agent: "Now that we've got that settled, I'll need you to take me to the transmitter immediately. I need to see the room and have access to everything in it."

Coordinator: "Okay no problem." He looked at all the agents and added, "Could you guys be careful with that? I don't want any viruses or cookies."

They all stared at him again, not hiding the fact that they thought he was a moron for trying to look tough in a situation that was clearly over his head and beyond what he could truly grasp.

Coordinator: "Carry on." He cleared his throat and began to walk away. The lead FBI agent and another man followed behind him. If they could have seen the coordinator's face they would have seen that he was so freaked out by the situation that he didn't know what to do. He had his hands shoved into his pockets and was clenching his fists, trying to gain some composure. He'd just surrendered all control of the television station under his command to the FBI. All he could think about was that his career was over and he was no where's near ready for an early retirement. He still had things to do, the kids college to finish paying for, and to buy that perfect little piece of land where he could move some day and live in solitude and quiet, and definitely no television.

Chapter Twelve:
Perception

Deciding it was time to walk toward the old, startling woman, Shane took Emily's hand and the two began to make their way over to her. As they walked toward the table, something caught their attention to the right of them. They looked and were surprised to see that a merry-go-round had shown up nearby.

"That wasn't there before," Shane commented.

"I sure didn't see it. It looks fun though."

"Not now, we have to go talk to...." Shane stopped mid-sentence. He looked back to where the old woman was and she was no longer there. Instead, there was a younger woman there who had a picnic feast spread out on the table. She had some children with her, who were all running toward the merry-go-round, laughing and shouting, ready to play. They looked so happy.

Then the woman looked to Shane and Emily and waved, smiling warmly. She definitely looked like she'd been expecting them and was not the least bit surprised to see them. She wore a linen dress that was fitted around the waist and stopped at her knee, flaring out about three inches. Her skin was tanned, her shape petite, and her hair was long and brunette, held back by a butterfly clip that accented her caramel colored highlights. Her sandals were flat and white with brown stones that covered the strap. What was surprising to see was that her toe nails were painted black, making for an odd contrast to the prim and proper woman they saw in front of them.

"Hello, how do you do? My name is Kate Odayle." She extended her hand to Shane, who shook it cautiously. He clearly didn't know what to make of the situation and was not going to let his guards down.

"Nice to meet you," he replied apprehensively. "I'm Shane and this is my daughter Emily."

"Hi Emily," Kate said, smiling at her so warmly, almost as if she was her own child or something like that. She extended her hand out to Emily, who took it.

"Nice to meet you, too," Emily said. Shane looked at her and could tell that she really liked this lady immediately.

Kate pointed to the table, which was filled with piles of food. "You know, this food is going to waste. Please help yourself."

"Why do you have so much food for just three people?" Shane asked suspiciously.

"Why, it's for five people, not three," Kate replied, unfazed by his direct questioning and obvious distrust.

Then Shane looked at Emily and saw that she was walking over toward the merry-go-round. "Don't go over there, Emily. Stay close to me!"

"Why? It looks like fun. I want to play," Emily challenged.

"Here. Now!" Shane commanded her like she was in the military with him and she rolled her eyes and headed back over to her dad.

"I don't see why…" she began.

Shane looked at her and leaned down. "We stay together unless I say differently. Got it?"

"Got it," Emily said, but not before rolling her eyes once more.

Meanwhile, Kate was watching the interaction and didn't seem to mind at all. She was still smiling as cheerily as if there were no cares in the world. Well, maybe there weren't in the painting world, but Shane was very aware that he and Emily were not going to get two million dollars by riding a merry-go-round and eating a scrumptious feast in the middle of a field. There was more to it, although it was getting harder to recall. Time and thought seemed so different here. He couldn't quite figure it out, but he was aware of it nonetheless.

Kate said, "It's a beautiful day today. I can't believe it. It's been raining all week. It finally cleared up yesterday. We were getting a bit stir crazy. It's just lovely to be out and about, don't you agree?"

"Mmm…hmmm," Emily said. She looked toward the merry-go-round and shook her head. Were her eyes playing tricks on her? "Look Daddy, it's raining over there, but not here. What's going on with that?"

"I don't know, but we are getting too distracted. Come on. We've got to get going," he said.

"Wait, don't forget to eat something," Kate said.

"Not now," Shane said.

He didn't see it, but Emily grabbed a crème puff and a few of the fresh strawberries from the table of food and put them into her pocket. They looked good and she was not about to pass them up. Kate looked at her and smiled, giving her a thumb up. She snuck her one back.

Then Shane grabbed Emily's hand, something he found himself doing more frequently in this peculiar land. He began to walk over toward the white winged horse, which he now saw was actually a pegasus. They may not be real in the world he was used to, but in this painting, or whatever it truly was, they clearly could exist.

"We've got to help that...pegasus," Emily began. "That's a pegasus. That's so cool! Daddy, we've got to help it. The tiger is scaring it."

"That tiger could just decide to pounce on us and then there'd be nothing we could do."

"Why wouldn't it have done it before if it was going to?" Emily asked. "I really think this painting wants us to think what may normally be scary in our world should be scary here. Only I don't think it is."

"You're sounding more like Einstein giving a theory than my ten year old daughter," Shane said. He looked at Emily, trying to evaluate if this was just a fantasy her mind concocted or if it had some validity to it. "I have to admit, you may be on to something. You're getting too smart!"

"I'm just like you that means," Emily said.

"More like your mother probably, but that's a good thing," Shane added.

Emily smiled and felt for the necklace she had put on earlier. She clearly liked having that feeling that her mother was close-by. The necklace reminded her of that.

Shane and Emily broke out into a run and it caught the tiger's attention. It began to pace, which made the pegasus do the same thing.

Emily said, "Its teeth are long."

"They sure are. Bigger than a hunting knife. Let's just get past that tiger and get to the pegasus, Em."

"What then?"

"I honestly have no idea. We'll assess the situation further when it comes."

As they moved past the tiger they noticed that it had somehow been tied up again, keeping it just out of reach of the pegasus. How had that happened? Was someone watching them? They'd just seen it earlier walking through the field. Or, worse yet, were there two tigers?

"I don't like this," Emily said.

"Me either," Shane said. Then he put his finger up to his lips so he could listen. They were at the edge of the woods now and he was trying to see if there were any other eyes on them aside from the pegasus and tiger's. He'd turned around and saw that merry-go-round and Kate were gone. It was just them again.

The tiger began to lunge more aggressively now, making the stake in the ground become looser with each forceful thrust. Emily stared at it, her body growing stiffer.

"I think I may have been wrong, Daddy. I think that tiger does want to get us."

"We can't worry about that now, kiddo. Let's get to that pegasus and try to get out of here as quick as possible. Got it?"

Emily nodded her head yes. Her heart was pounding so rapidly that it felt like someone was pounding on her chest with mallets. It echoed in her ears and made it hard for her to hear anything at all.

Shane kept walking forward slowly, keeping his eyes connected to the pegasus. He saw that the one leg of the winged horse was tied up, making it so it couldn't go anywhere.

"Easy," he said softly. He leaned down and began to untie the rope from around the pegasus's hind leg, having to work to get the knot out.

"Daddy, the tiger's almost loose," Emily whispered.

Shane glanced over and began to work on the knot more aggressively. He finally loosened the knot.

"Come on, let's get on," Shane said.

Emily didn't move, seemingly frozen in place, and Shane looked over to see the tiger lunging toward them. It had broken free. Shane hopped up on the winged horse aggressively and grabbed Emily, moving her out of the way in just a knick of time. He lifted her up with one arm, throwing her on the back of the pegasus, and they took off as quickly as they could. Shane held into the mane of the pegasus as tightly as possible and Emily was holding on around his waist with clenched fists grabbing the material of his shirt.

"Come on girl, fly. You can do it," Shane urged.

The tiger was running next to the pegasus, easily keeping pace with it and starting to lunge toward it, pouncing and trying to knock off Shane and Emily any way it could.

In the distance, there was a hazy patch. Rain was falling around it, but it seemed to be clear, almost like it was filled with smoke or something.

Emily screamed and Shane turned his head just enough to see that the tiger had scratched her leg and it was bleeding. He kicked back with the heel of his commando style boots and delivered a swift kick to the tiger's jaw, which temporarily startled it.

Shane held on to the mane even more tightly after that and called out to the pegasus as if it understood his every word. "We've got to make that jump."

The hazy circle got closer and closer, the pegasus moved more quickly, and the tiger had regained its wits and was running right alongside them.

Then, it happened. The tiger leapt through the circle first and there was no time to stop. The pegasus followed with Shane and Emily bouncing about on its back, holding on for dear life as it went through the portal in the painting.

The tiger wasn't confused, or the pegasus either, but Shane was. He looked around and saw sand everywhere, reminding him of those hard days in the desert when he was in service. It was the only thing he could see everywhere. Then the pegasus took flight into the sky and Shane looked back, seeing that the tiger had stopped. It had lost out on its meal and the chase.

"What are we going to do now?" Em asked.

Shane turned around to see his daughter as much as he could and saw that she was very pale.

"We've got to stop the bleeding on that scratch. That's what we've got to do."

"Okay, Daddy."

Then a group of trees appeared below. Shane had no idea if it was an actual oasis or a mirage, but he had to go and find out. Emily needed attention and he wasn't going to let anyone or anything stop him from giving it to her.

Chapter Thirteen:
Chinese Snake Fish

Two days before Jennifer's start date

Nick Kashan was standing in it waist high, enjoying the refreshment it provided. He turned to Candy. "Come on; get in here. It's nice."

From the pick-up truck, Candy Allen was pulling out two beers from the cooler. "Hold on, I'm coming."

She tossed down a shot and then made her way toward Nick with two beers. She set them down and looked at him, peeling off her shorts and tank top, revealing her checkered two-piece swimsuit, to which Nick gave a whistle of approval. Candy posed for him with all sorts of different angles and then made her way to the edge of the lake.

Nick dipped his head into the water and whipped it back up, shaking the water from his hair. It splashed, making small ripples in the water.

Candy walked over to him, smiling coyly at him. "How is it that we always manage to end up here alone, Nick Kashan? I swear it's on purpose." She reached out, handing him his beer.

"Just works out that way for me. I'm not complaining. There are certain things we can do that are much more fun when we have some privacy."

"Yeah, we sure don't get it at either of houses, do we?"

"It'd help if your parents liked me."

"It's not like your parents are a fan of mine either," Candy replied.

Nick smiled, holding his hand out and then winking flirtatiously at Candy. She knew what he wanted and she certainly didn't mind herself.

Her mood suddenly changed and she swatted at his arm. "Oh yeah. You know that reminds me. I'm still mad at you."

Ignoring the slap, Nick yelled, "What the hell man? Something just bit the shit out of my leg." He looked around and saw something moving.

Candy screamed. "What is that?"

"Get out of the water now!" Blood began flooding the water and the two started to move toward the shore as quickly as they could.

Nick turned to see a large bizarre fish jump out of the water and lunge toward his face, latching on to his ear.

Candy yelled, "Nick!" He lost his balance and his body toppled back into the water. She reached out, trying to grip his arm to pull him out. The same fish swam up and took a chunk out of her lower leg. She slipped and fell face first into the water, hitting her head on a rock, and got instantly dizzy. She couldn't get up. In the next instant, they were both are surrounded by Chinese Snake Fish of all sizes. There was nothing they could do and eventually they surrendered to the fight, unable to ward off any attack. There was no evidence of them ever being there, aside from fading red blood spots in the water and the vehicle that they drove to the lake in.

* * * *

Jennifer wasn't very eager for her new job to start, but she made her way out to Caballo Lake, where she'd be working to find out more about what she'd be doing and how alien species were linked to Caballo Lake. However, it was nice that she wasn't going to be trapped in some office. It would have been better if the place she was at wasn't so isolated, and at times, not able to hold a cell phone call without dropping it. That really made her anxious because if Amanda needed her, she may not be there as quickly as she could be. *Just keep thinking about the pay,* she reminded herself.

She pulled up and saw an empty truck sitting there. She looked around and the lake, but nobody could be seen. They must have been on the far side of it or something, maybe hidden behind some of the grass around the edges.

As her instructions had said, there was a small boat with an even smaller motor waiting at the edge of the lake for Jennifer. She got into the boat and decided to row it toward the center of the lake instead of using the motor. Then she could use up some energy and not have to worry about getting too antsy about sitting in a boat for the day. Honestly, she didn't get why this would be such a good paying job, considering it involved doing nothing aside from observing. You could have paid some undergraduate minimum wage to do it. They probably would have done it for free, actually.

Every once in awhile, she'd look at the lake through her binoculars, but didn't really see anything notable at all. The sun was still beating down on the top of the water, creating optical illusions that made it hard to see if anything was happening. She reached down to her cell phone to see if she had reception. She'd missed four calls. Her phone hadn't rung because she was roaming. She opened it up, put it on speaker, and began to listen to her messages.

One was Stacy. That was nice. The other three were from debt collectors and she deleted those immediately, not wanting to hear them tell her what she already knew. In a few weeks' time, after she'd stopped her house from going into foreclosure and collected her two million dollars, she'd be able to pay off those guys and never hear from them again. Good riddance.

Sitting there and staring out at nothing, Jennifer was trying to process the fact that she was actually in some sort of game, but living her life as she would have if she didn't enter it. It was confusing, almost disorienting, and there was no logical explanation that made sense. Although she was messed up emotionally she was still a smart woman. Why couldn't she figure this out? Was anyone watching her? That was her other thought right now.

She looked around, suddenly feeling edgy about the idea that someone could be watching her and she could not see them. Some movement in the water caught her attention and she saw the water begin to ripple. It was as if someone was throwing small rocks into it. Then a patch of red began to grow.

Jennifer paddled to the patch of red in the water and stopped the boat. "Is that blood," she mumbled.

She baited a hook from the pole that was in her boat and cast the fishing pole out into the water. Nothing took the bait. She tried again and this time there was a nibble on the line. She tugged, snaring the hook into it and reeled in the line. When she saw what she'd caught she wasn't sure what to make of it. It was a small baby fish that had a head like a snake. It was very unusual and something she'd never seen before; definitely not something native to the region. With gloves on, she'd put it into a bag filled with water, watching it flail around, trying to release itself.

Then Jennifer put the pole back in the water, wondering what other odd things she might find. She had no takers for her next two casts. Finally, after the third cast there was a bite on the pole. She began to reel it in and there was a lot of resistance. "This is a big one," she said, tugging harder to conquer the fish on the other end. She planted her feet on the small bench in front of her, trying to leverage her weight against the big fish that was fighting for all it was worth to not cooperate with her.

The boat began sliding forward and Jennifer countered, tugging with all the strength she had and finally reeled the fish in. It felt like she was on a deep sea fishing adventure, not a casual fishing observation trip on the lake.

Staring at the fish she was shocked to see that it was like the small one, a fish with a snake head. She'd have to look it up and see what kind of fish it was at the end of the day. Without a doubt, it was an alien species and was certainly powerful and ferocious.

After having to fight to take the hook out of its mouth, Jennifer opened up a cooler and tossed the fish into it. After she closed the lid, she could hear it thrashing about in there, making a lot of noise and literally rocking the boat as a result.

She breathed heavily, a bit startled by the strength of the fish, and began to make her way back to shore. She didn't want to be on that small boat with that fish. Plus, she wanted to find out exactly what type of fish it was. It looked like she had an interesting mystery on her hands.

A half hour later, everything was loaded up in the truck she'd driven out there and she was on her way to the lab where she would be working when she wasn't on the lake observing.

With large blue gloves on, Jennifer sat at a large desk, facing a wall. There was an opening underneath, giving her legs enough room to stretch out. A filing cabinet was next to her, serving as a table top for the silver platter that had three cutting utensils on it. In the corner was a 52" flat screen monitor. She was researching online and had a reference manual open. She couldn't believe what she thought she'd discovered though. It made no sense. The baby fish and the adult one that she'd caught seemed to be Chinese Snake Fish. It was a rare and unique breed, certainly not native to North America. How did it get here? Someone had planted it and it had taken to its new habitat with a fierce aggression.

Losing track of time, Jennifer pulled up images of everything she could find about the fish, trying to learn more, and, more importantly – get an accurate picture so she could present the problem to her bosses. It was definitely a significant problem.

She zoomed in and focused on a single fish egg. The mother snake-fish was swimming in a nearby tank, still making its presence known with its explosive, volatile actions.

Jennifer had to admit that she was impressed with the lab they'd provided her to do the research. It had state of the art everything. It was impressive and these snake-fish were most unusual. They gave her the creeps, but fascinated her at the same time. They'd be an interesting challenge to figure out.

Jennifer happened to catch her watch in her peripheral and looked at it. She was running late. It was time to get home. The challenge of figuring out the fish would have to wait until tomorrow.

She jumped in her car, leaving behind the truck the lab had provided her, and made her way toward Stacy's house to get Amanda.

Stacy was standing out in the driveway and little Clark was resting on her hip. Jennifer smiled and waved.

"So, how was it?"

"Both boring and interesting," Jennifer said.

"You realize that doesn't make any sense, right?"

"I know. I'll explain later. It won't be very interesting for you, unless you've developed a taste for biology."

"No, I haven't. I'm just waiting for the babysitter," Stacy said.

"Why? Where you going and why didn't you ask me to watch the kids?"

"With your new job and all..." Stacy paused. Jennifer knew that while they were best friends, Stacy worried about her state of mind sometimes. Amanda was old enough to understand and manage it, but Jennifer didn't want to put too much on her plate until she became more, let's just say, balanced again.

"So, you still didn't answer," Jennifer continued. "Where are you going?"

"David and I are going out to eat."

"Seriously?" Jennifer was absolutely shocked to hear that Stacy would be going out to eat with him. Even though they weren't technically divorced, it seemed that way. Plus, they rarely got along despite both of them trying to. Their situation was just too tense for them. They both took a bit of misery to ensure the kids were OK. Well, Stacy did, anyway. Dave seemed to maintain his life pretty well.

"Yes, we've decided to see if we can maybe work things out."

"What about your suspicions?"

"Well, they were never proven. It's just dinner. Don't jump the gun," Stacy said.

"Okay. Have fun, Stacy. You know I only want you to be happy, right?"

"I know."

"So, where's Amanda?" Jennifer asked.

"She and Christy are doing homework in her bedroom."

Just as Jennifer began to walk down the hallway, Stacy tugged on her arm. "You know, I don't get what's going on. We're in a game, but we're living our normal lives. What's the deal?"

"Honestly, I don't know, but it's only been a day and I feel like I've forgotten that I even went to Rhode Island for that meeting."

"I know what you mean," Stacy said.

"I thought maybe it was my new medicine, it just kind of made me forget…or at least not dwell on things so much, Stacy. But if you're feeling the same way, maybe it's something else."

"Well, who knows?"

A few minutes later, Jennifer and Amanda were leaving as the doorbell was ringing. The babysitter had shown up. Right behind her was David. Apparently he'd given her a ride.

Jennifer smiled, looking at the teenager, who seemed to be more of a twenty-something than a high school girl. She looked over at Amanda, realizing she was definitely in no hurry for her to grow up.

"Talk later," Jennifer called out. Then she and Amanda were off.

Chapter Fourteen:
Calm and Calculating

Tayyip was pleased to see how his little game was unfolding. Everything had been working brilliantly and two people he truly despised were on their way to creating their own destruction, feeling the pain of loss like what he'd already experienced. Only they would never get a chance for revenge.

"Show me the second camera angle for Braff," Tayyip said, tapping his fingers on his desk.

He panned in and saw that the young Emily had snuck some of the food into her pocket. When he saw how deeply the tiger has scratched her leg, he clapped his hands, smiling all the while. Yes, that Shane was good, but that's what made him such a worthy adversary in this game within The Land of Paintings. Still, in the end, he could not win.

"Sir, we just received a new shipment of fish. Where would you like me to put them?"

"You may set them in the tank over there," Tayyip said, pointing to a tank on the wall. It was contained within a picture and within that picture was Caballo Lake.

The one thing that perplexed Tayyip about seeing his plans unfold was how utterly dull Jennifer Koppell was. She seemed to have no fight in her and it reminded him of how she looked as she did nothing that day his life had changed forever. Yet, she was among the smartest and elite of the US Government once upon a time, according to the military and FBI databases, anyway. He'd have to toss some things her way to liven up the show – generate some excitement. After all, he didn't want to bore his audience. Yes, all eyes in the world were glued on the impromptu reality show that had invaded the Super Bowl.

Chapter Fifteen:
Looking for a Lead

The situation was urgent inside the command room as the FBI began to get to the bottom of the hijacking of the television stations airwaves and to figure out who the people were that were a part of the impromptu broadcast.

Lead FBI agent: "Scan in on those two people and get all of the information you can. We need to find out who they are, who's hijacked this signal, and what the connection is."

Agent O: "You think there is one, boss?"

Lead FBI agent: "It's the most logical, but we're obviously dealing with a well connected, but sick individual."

Agent Z: "I think I have something of interest, a telephone call."

Lead FBI Agent: "Let's see it."

The agent watched the telephone call and had the audio controller zoom in and enhance the image quality to get a better idea. No details could be taken for granted and they sure couldn't afford to overlook anything. It was all happening so fast and every minute was critical.

Lead FBI Agent: "Any info on whom the call was to yet?"

Agent O: "It appears to be to a Tayyip Nafisi. The odd part is that it loops back to the station. They've jammed the signals, making it impossible to get a true trace."

Lead FBI Agent: "Run that name. It sounds familiar, but I can't think of from where."

Agent Z: "Yes sir."

With a fresh pot of coffee delivered, the agents all kept reviewing footage and putting possible ideas up on a bulletin board, trying to make a connection about everything that made sense.

Agent Z: "Sir, I got a report in on Tayyip Nafisi."

Lead FBI agent: "Hand it over."

The lead agent looked at the report and his eyes became alert with recognition immediately. The story of what happened to Tayyip Nafisi was one that everyone had been aware of at the time because it had really marred the military's reputation, as well as put a bunch of top tier officials in the hot seat.

Lead FBI agent: "I didn't know he was back in the States. When did he get here?"

Agent Z: "About a year ago it seems, sir."

Lead FBI agent: "Get me the names of the soldiers that were involved with his case pronto. I need to know where each one is, their status, and as much information as I can get."

Agent O: "Already on that, sir. Here it is."

Agent O handed the lead agent the report and he looked through it and then glanced to the television monitor, and then back again.

Lead FBI agent: "These people haven't fared so well, have they? It looks like Issac Rainnek is dead; according to the computer, Jennifer Koppell is deceased. That leaves just Shane Braff and Dan Markel alive."

Agent Z: "Markel is living in rural Maryland. Braff lives with his daughter in Hermosa Beach, California."

Lead FBI agent: "Send agents to their houses right away and put them into protective custody if they are there."

Agent Z: "I don't think that Braff is there, sir. I just received a picture and voice confirmation that it is him and his daughter inside The Land of the Paintings."

Agent O: "Who's the other one then?"

Lead FBI agent: "I'll be damned. I think it is Jennifer Koppell. Well, well, well...she's looking pretty good for supposedly being dead."

Agent Z: "How could that have happened?"

Lead FBI agent: "I don't know, but find out where she is at in that damn television show and get people there pronto. I don't know if she's in some high tech painting or actually back at her home. It's a weird scenario…a real mind game."

Agent Z: "Yes, sir."

Lead FBI agent: "Now, how's it going with unlocking this signal?"

Agent O: "Not good. We can't figure it out, can't even find a flaw in the plan."

Lead FBI agent: "That's impossible. Every plan has a flaw, something they didn't anticipate. We'll just have to find out what this one is. Tayyip Nafisi, what are you up to?"

Chapter Sixteen:
The Sands of Time

Making their way to the small oasis in the sandy desert, Shane was exhausted and worried about Emily, who, thanks to losing blood rapidly, was looking paler than ever.

"How are you going to stop the bleeding, Daddy?" she whispered.

"I'll have to find some mud and wrap it in some of these palm leaves. That should stop it long enough to clot properly."

"I feel so hungry all of a sudden," Emily said.

"I'm sorry. We don't have any food, kiddo. We'll figure that out after we get the bleeding stopped, okay?"

Emily nodded her head slowly, trying to focus on Shane. It looked like there was three of him staring back at her. She held her hand out to see if she could touch the right one, but realized she didn't have the strength.

"You stay still and quiet while I scour this little patch of turf to get what I need," Shane said. Then he took off, trying to collect things as quickly as possible. The pegasus stood still; seemingly calm and thankful for the reprieve.

As Shane looked around, he was feeling so helpless, not being able to protect his daughter better. A tiger!

What type of national television show set up a scenario where two people almost get mauled by a tiger? Words from Mathew Lengyel echoed in his mind: completely harmless. Yeah, right!

Ten minutes later he came back and looked at Emily. She was sound asleep with some white powder around her lips. Next to her on the ground were the stems from two strawberries. She must have snuck some of that food from the past picture. Well, he didn't have time to worry about that now.

Shane got to work, creating a paste with the mud and slathering it on the scrawny leg of his daughter. It was good and thick, which stopped the blood from seeping out. Next, he wrapped it in some fern leaves that he'd found. They were wider and softer than the palm tree leaves. Now he just needed one more layer of protection...something to hold it all on.

He looked around and saw nothing aside from the white t-shirt he had on underneath his shirt. He took his shirt off and then his t-shirt, tugged at the sleeve and easily ripped the seams, and then ripped it once again. It was a good fit for being makeshift.

"Okay, you're going to have to wake up now, Emily," Shane said, gently shaking his daughter.

"I'm so tired."

"I know. You're going to have to get onto the back of the pegasus with me and hold on tightly, not letting go."

"Okay, Daddy."

Once they were on the move again, Shane was surprised to see a town in the distance, not too far away. It looked small and almost like a Normal Rockwell painting, except it was in the middle of a vast desert.

Shane wanted to reach that town before the sunset, but it was challenging to do. He was afraid Emily was going to slide off. Unfortunately, this made it difficult for him to get a good grip on the horse's mane. They would have to take it slowly.

Emily kept sleeping, not able to stay awake. Although she was so slight of frame, her dead weight was very difficult to manage, even for Shane's strong arms. Plus, the pegasus was slowing down, showing its exhaustion from being on the ground for so long.

Shane realized that it was strange that the pegasus seemed to instinctually know what he wanted it to do. It certainly wasn't trained to follow his commands, but yet it knew. He began to wonder if there was an element of truth to Emily's theory about the paintings being able to sense their fears and what they'd do, adjusting and reacting to it in an instant. It was an eerie thought and it made Shane clearly uncomfortable. It was Big Brother to the extreme.

"Stop! I have to throw up," Emily suddenly announced.

Shane tried to stop the unicorn, but this time it

wouldn't listen. It began to go faster, trying to take off into the sky. The resistance Shane gave was enough to stop it, but it broke into a full out gallop, charging over the sandy hills.

"Daddy, I'm going to be sick," Emily repeated.

"Just hold on. It won't stop." No sooner were the words out than Shane realized the reason. The winds began picking up and the sand began to fly through the air, pelting against their bodies like small razor blades. The ruthless assault stung their skins badly.

"Ow!" Emily screamed.

"Keep your head down," Shane yelled, taking in a mouthful of sand in the process.

He looked around and couldn't believe it. There was a sandstorm coming toward them. It looked like it was a mile across. There was no way they were going to escape it, but they had to find some place to shelter from its fury.

Just then, the pegasus stopped, rearing its legs, sending Shane and Emily flying off its back. They landed in a painful thud on the sandy hill.

Shane lost his breath temporarily, but managed to remain calm, knowing he'd get it back sooner. He crawled over to Emily, who was now on all fours, vomiting furiously, her thin frame heaving and convulsing.

"We've got to get out of here, baby. I don't care if you puke while I'm carrying you, but we are close enough to that village that we may – just may – make it."

It took every bit of mental fortitude he had, but Shane kept moving forward against the whipping wind and pelting sand, running toward the village as fast as he could, not letting any amount of pain stop him. His face stung and he suspected that he had tiny abrasions all over it, but it didn't matter. His motivation to save his daughter numbed his pain. He swore he'd always protect her and he wasn't going to let anything stop him from doing just that.

Making it to the small main street of the village, Shane ran up to the first house he saw. It was a wooden house that barely had any paint on it, having been sandblasted off from previous sandstorms. He knocked on the door loudly. No one answered.

There was no time to wait. He could feel the storm breathing down his neck. He turned the door knob. Amazingly, the house was unlocked. The second he swung open the door, the wind stopped and the sand dropped down to the ground. Just like that, the storm was over, but something more frightening was about to begin.

Shane looked down into Emily's eyes. They looked so vacant, like she was a million miles away. She was staring back at him though. "My throat's burning," Emily said weakly.

"We'll get you some water," Shane said. He was trying to think of how a tiger scratch could cause such a reaction and then he realized it wasn't the scratch at all. It was that damn food she'd eaten. It was poisoned. So much for fruitful bliss.

Chapter Seventeen:
Girl's Night Out

Jennifer had actually gotten off work early, going to talk with Stacy for a bit. It felt nice not having to rush out the door to get Amanda home. As Stacy helped Christy with something in another room, Jennifer sat in the kitchen, looking at Clark. The baby had made a huge mess with his oatmeal. He somehow got it all over him, his high chair, and the floor. It made her smile though. She wished that she'd had the opportunity to see those special moments with Amanda. That hadn't been the case with her, however, because first she had been serving and then she'd mentally checked out, whether or not she liked to believe it. The one good thing was that the new red pills she'd been taking seemed to help. Everything did seem more manageable, the sleep walking had all but disappeared, and she was able to get through a day without being in excruciating emotional pain. So, all in all, things were looking up.

When Stacy came back in the kitchen, Jennifer looked up and smiled, but then her attention went right back to Clark.

"You know, Jennifer, I was thinking that we need to have a girls' night out. It would be so much fun and both of us could use a little break," Stacy offered.

"You have just gotten back into full swing of re-entry into marital bliss. Why do you need a break?" Jennifer asked. She realized that her words sounded harsh, but that wasn't their intention. "Sorry, I didn't mean it like that."

"Well, we still have plenty of work to do. It's funny how I forgot about how many hours he works sometimes. Whether he's here or not, my life really remains unchanged. How's that for sad?"

"Pretty sad," Jennifer agreed. "I'm not sure about going out though. I'm not sure if I'm ready. Plus, I don't want to meet any new assholes. Besides, who'd watch the kids?"

"What a stream of lame excuses," Stacy said. "We're not talking marriage or even a serious relationship. We're talking having some fun, acting carefree for a night so we can remember that we are still young, despite all that we've been through."

"It's not that I don't get what you're saying, but I hardly think that we'll be able to find a babysitter at this late hour," Jennifer said.

"Let me see," Stacy said. Jennifer wanted to retort with the fact that she was still broke and yet to receive a paycheck, but she didn't say it out loud. Her pride didn't allow her to.

"What would we do anyway?"

"I have a great idea," Stacy said. "We can go to my boss's party in the city tonight. It would be perfect. Not too crazy or wild, but interesting. He's quite a unique man, that's for sure. Just give me a minute." She left the room with her cell phone and came back about five minutes later. "Be ready to go in an hour. You can wear anything of mine you like and freshen up here."

"Oh, okay," Jennifer said. The one thing, besides the same dress size, that she had in common with Stacy was that they were both determined people. When they set their minds to something, they usually got their way. Plus, Jennifer didn't want to admit it, but it really was time that she met someone new...a living breathing male to have a conversation with. Talking to Issac's haunting memory wasn't cutting it any longer and she knew that he, more than anyone, would have wanted her to experience love, or at least a good relationship, again. It had been three years, but it seemed like an eternity.

As Jennifer went to raid Stacy's closet she realized just how out of touch she was with clothes that a woman on the prowl might wear. Everything looked either too provocative or too frumpy. Finally, she settled on a cashmere sweater and a black pencil skirt. She just happened to have a pair of black pumps in her trunk that would great with it.

"Well, how do I look?" Jennifer asked, putting her arms out.

"Wow-eee!" Stacy exclaimed.

"Mom, you look beautiful," Amanda said, coming around the corner.

"Thanks, honey," Jennifer said, looking at her

daughter. Then she suddenly felt nervous about going out and was fearful that her anxiety would get the best of her. She went over to her purse and pulled out her bottle of pills.

Stacy watched her and came over. "It's going to be okay," she said, touching her arm softly. She loved that Jennifer was finally getting better after her brother's death and was glad the magical red pills helped, but she was fearful that she was becoming dependent on them instead of working out the demons that haunted her. However, now she was rebounding back to the person she'd used to be. It was nice to have her best friend back.

"You know. I haven't had a chance to thank you for picking up the slack and bringing the girls home from school. I know that I'd been doing that far too long, but now with this job, it just isn't always possible."

"You'll have to tell me more about how that's going when we head into the city."

"Sounds like a great plan."

There was a knock on the front door and Casey Leannier, as responsible and serious of a sixteen year old that anyone had ever seen, stood there.

"Thanks for coming on such short notice, Casey" Stacy said.

"No problem. What are the rules tonight and when can I tell my parents I'll be home?"

"We shouldn't be late," Stacy said, turning to Jennifer to smile.

Jennifer immediately liked Casey, thinking she would be excellent military material. Sure, she looked cute with her high ponytail, tennis skirt, polo shirt, and sneakers, but, clearly, she was serious about everything she did. The kids all came out and Christy introduced Amanda.

When it was time to go, Jennifer hesitated again. It had become all too real.

Stacy laughed. "Come on. They will be okay."

Jennifer said, "Okay give me a hug the both of you. Um...be good. Don't give her a hard time."

Christy said, "We won't."

Amanda said, "Have fun, Mommy."

"Awe, honey. I will try to for you, okay."

"Don't worry. I'll have fun," Amanda said. With that, she went down the hallway ready to enjoy some more fun with Christy. Jennifer had already left from her perspective and she was set to enjoy a night of fun with her cousin. It was certainly much better time compared to doing military drills in her backyard.

Stacy was already in her car, starting it up when Jennifer got out there. She motioned for her to hurry. They needed to get out of there before Jennifer changed her mind.

Now it was time to get to the posh El Paso suburb, where Stacy's employer's house stood. It sounded like the man had quite the house, as would make sense with a high profile, successful managing partner in a law firm.

"All right, spill the dirt on your new job that takes up so much time in a given day," Stacy said, turning down the radio so she could hear.

"Gosh, it's a dirty job but somebody's got to do it. I'm just glad that Amanda's smiling more. I know she wants me to take her to school again and hopefully I'll be able to soon."

"Wonderful, but I don't mind doing it," Stacy said.

"Your boss doesn't mind?"

"No," Stacy replied all too quickly. Then she changed the subject. "So, your new medicine is working well for you, huh?"

"It is. Nothing haunts me so much anymore. I've got to tell you though...I have this nagging feeling that I've forgotten about something."

"Like what?" Stacy asked.

"No idea," Jennifer confessed.

"Well, it can't be that important then," Stacy replied.

What neither of them realized was that they had indeed forgotten something...something important that had slowly faded from their memories. It all stemmed from a little meeting they'd had in Rhode Island just over a week ago.

Stacy took a breath and kept her eyes on the road, wanting to bring up a subject that she knew Jennifer would be delicate about. Whatever she'd possibly forgotten, this was one thing she could not forget. Neither of them could forget. "So, you're doing better and still not mourning over Issac? He was a great brother and we all miss him, but we have to keep moving on, right?"

Jennifer looked at her with a blank stare. "I'm doing okay."

"I'm sorry, I shouldn't have said that."

Jennifer said, "I should get a move on with my life, right? That's what everyone keeps telling me."

"Have you finished packing up his things?"

Jennifer turned to face Stacy. "No, no I haven't."

"You should let me do it. I mean, it's the least I can do. I can come over while you are at work and do it. Then you won't have to worry about it or go through any more than you have to."

Jennifer sighed, "Thanks but…"

Stacy knew where she was headed and stopped her. "You know I loved him too and now we have to take care of each other. Please let me do it." She reached over and touched Jennifer's hand.

"I know how you felt about him too, Stacy. It's something I just have to face on my own, that's all."

"Well, this isn't a good way to start off our girls' night." Stacy sighed. "We've got to drop the baggage and move on with things. My attempt at making things better again clearly isn't going to work and you have to deal with things in your own way. It is what it is and there's nothing we can do besides support each other, right?"

"Right," Jennifer agreed. "Well, now that we've diffused, maybe we can relax a bit and have some fun."

Stacy clearly needed to vent because she began to talk again. "I just can't believe I spent half my life wrapped up into one man, knew it wasn't working, tried to make it work again, and have found myself back at square one."

"What has he done now?"

"Haven't seen him enough for him to do anything today. It's not what he's done now; it's what he did then, and is still doing. I swear I hate him."

"Don't say that. He's the father of your kids, if nothing else. Hating him won't help. But...you definitely feel the attempt to get back together was a bad idea?" Jennifer asked.

"I don't know...I think so. What I don't want to do is

relive it all over again. Plus, explaining it to Christy again may be just too much. Thankfully Clark's too little to realize." Stacy stopped short of saying anything else. She loved her baby so much, but he was also a representation of her weakness for her husband, as he was the product of a tryst with him one night. He was loved, but not created from the 'ideal love,' if that even existed.

"I'm sorry," Jennifer said. What a pair of friends they were. One was concerned about severing a relationship and one was worried about never finding an opportunity at love again.

"I wasn't going to say anything because I didn't want you to think I'd completely lost my marbles, but I told him to leave again today. He did it, but I'm completely terrified to tell Christy that again."

"Stacy, you'll find the right way in your own time. I know you will. And…not to drag you down, but you realize she's smart enough and old enough to figure it out on her own, right?"

Stacy shrugged her shoulders and breathed in deeply. "I wish I had a cigarette to calm my nerves down. Well, since I don't, I am glad we're getting out," Stacy said, attempting to change the subject again.

"Maybe I should drive. You can drive back," Jennifer offered. She saw how stressed Stacy was and it made her feel bad.

"Don't worry. We'll make it there in one piece," Stacy said, pressing down on the gas pedal and thrusting the car onto the freeway at full speed. All Jennifer could do was hold her heart and say a quick prayer that her friend would be good.

* * * *

Tayyip was sitting in a chair, staring at his reflection in the mirror in front of him. His face was covered in white makeup that had been applied with a small airbrush. It looked natural, perfectly complementary to an attractive white male and what his skin tones may look like. He was every bit the man he was portraying that night. And what a delightful night it was going to be. Tayyip felt so excited to be participating in his little game. Really, it was the only way to make the utterly mundane life of Jennifer Koppell more bearable. He despised people who wallowed in pain and did nothing to change it. Look at him? He'd truly lost everything, yet you didn't see him sulking in the shadows. He was being proactive about it.

He was humming a tune, while he stared at himself in the mirror, pausing and focusing on his facial expressions and mannerisms. "Would you like some more wine?" He spoke aloud and his accent immediately changed from its standard thick Iraqi one to a perfect Midwestern United States accent, showing no signs that he was from anywhere other than where he was pretending. Yes, he was brilliant and his ego allowed him to admit it quite effortlessly.

Shortly thereafter, guests began arriving at the house. He walked into the main room and greeted guests as they entered, smiling at them and shaking their hands. They all thought he was who he'd claimed to be; another sign of what he was capable of pulling off and also of how unaware so many Americans really were about their surroundings

Tayyip's 'home' was impeccable, filled with extravagant pictures hanging from the richly coated walls. The only echoes were the sounds of women's heels as they crossed the marble floor and made their way to the bar, toward another social group, or for appetizers.

Jennifer was in awe of the entire house, thinking it was absolutely exquisite. She took some time to do something she hadn't done in many years: view some art work. One picture in particular had caught her attention. She stared at it, holding a glass of wine. Art was her secret passion and something she knew a great deal about, despite having such an intense military career. If it hadn't been for her military family's background and father's insistence, she likely would have gone into the art field. Leave it to her family; most fathers discouraged their daughters from becoming warriors, but her father sent her in with a hearty farewell. Unfortunately, he died of the heart attack while she was serving.

She took a sip of wine and noticed someone watching her, but didn't think much of it. Her interest went back to the paintings, having lingered on this one for long enough. As she slowly walked around, observing all of them, she was drawn to another one that was of particular interest to her. She was also enjoying browsing the artwork more than throwing herself out there into awkward conversations with people she barely knew or didn't know at all.

Tayyip, who was known to everyone else as George Sterling, came up next to her. She glanced and smiled. "This can't be the original."

"Isn't it amazing how one stroke of imperfection can create a mountain of interest."

Jennifer tapped her wine glass with her forefinger. "Intriguing doubt and frustration."

"Who said it best?" George asked.

"Oates."

"Yes."

Jennifer looked at the man, drawn to the fact that he seemed to enjoy and understand art. "Hi, I am..."

"Jennifer."

"Yes," she said, surprised that he knew her name.

"I heard you introduce yourself earlier," Tayyip explained. "I'm George Sterling."

"Oh. It's nice to meet you. So, this is your house?" Jennifer asked.

"It is," he said.

"It's lovely," she said. She began to walk to another painting, fully aware that he was watching her. It shocked her that she felt excited. She couldn't recall the last time a man's gaze had lingered on her for longer than determining if she needed her meds adjusted.

"You like this one, I see."

"How can you tell?"

"I see it in your eyes."

Never being one who was too subtle, Jennifer commented. "Nice collection. Great taste. You must have a lot of money." She bit her lip, second guessing her abruptness. "I'm sorry," she added.

"It's okay. I work hard," he said.

"Certainly a law firm wouldn't give you all of this?" Jennifer asked

"That's only one part of my assets. I'm very...diverse...let's just say that. My interests are broad, making me a rather eclectic investor and collector alike, a bunch of odds and ends really." She stared at him, seducing a smile from him.

"Interesting. I didn't know there was so much to be made in...odds and ends."

George asked, "Would you like more?" He noticed that her glass was empty.

"Yes, that would be lovely," Jennifer said. "It's quite good."

He called over one of his servants. The man had on black pants, a white shirt, and a white tailored jacket that fell at waist level. "Thank you, Victor," George said after he'd filled both glasses.

"You're welcome, sir," Victor replied.

Jennifer heard some loud laughter and turned around to see Stacy entering the room. She was clearly enjoying herself and had been enjoying a few drinks...a few too many. It was always easy to tell with her because her blue eyes became more sparkly and intense, and her voice always got louder. She also got touchier. Now, she was smiling and carefree, just the opposite of the car ride over. "Jennifer, there you are. Come here. Oh, I'm sorry. Hi." She has one finger out, motioning for Jennifer to follow.

Jennifer said, "Excuse me."

"No problem, Jennifer." George watched her walk away and Jennifer could sense his eyes focused on her.

The two walked out of the room and Stacy began whispering in her ear. "This is my co-worker. He is so cute. He just joined the firm and he is single. Honey, watch out...oh." She spilled her drink on the floor. They look at each other and Stacy began laughing, which made Jennifer do the same.

They ended up sitting down with a group of people.

Everyone was so distinguished and eloquent, making Jennifer temporarily forget the baggage she was carrying inside for a bit. It did feel good.

Meanwhile, George and the new hottie from the firm, as Stacy had put it, Gregory Meskar, were seated a short distance away, watching Jennifer. She couldn't help but notice that George was there and she couldn't deny that she was interested in talking to him more. He was, by far, the most interesting person she'd met in a great while, and that included the person she looked at in the mirror every morning. She turned to Stacy and the others, excusing herself. None of them heard her because they were all wrapped up in office gossip.

Jennifer walked over to the two men.

George said, "Hello again, Jennifer."

"Hi."

"We were just discussing the...."

Gregory butted in. "I've seen you around."

"You have?" Jennifer asked, completely confused.

"To be frank, you are gorgeous I would love on take you on a date. Do you mind giving me your number?"

Jennifer looked back and forth between both men. What was going on? "No, I am really not interested."

"I need your number." Gregory pursued the issue.

"Oh, get it from Stacy."

"I have my phone right here. It's not a problem. I won't call when you're busy, three times a day, or anything like that."

"I'm sorry. I'm not use to this," Jennifer said, feeling her eyes stinging from the rush of tears. She wiped her eyes and began walking away. She couldn't even get out an apology for her behavior, but, as she left, she did notice the expression on George Sterling's face.

The fake George knew Jennifer Koppell's expressions very well. He got up and walked swiftly, matching her fast gate. "Excuse me, Jennifer."

"Yes," she said, not looking directly at him.

"I'm sorry. That was rude of Gregory. I don't like my guests to feel uncomfortable in my home."

"It's just me," she said. "I feel like I did something wrong."

She found Stacy, telling her they had to leave.

"Come on, Jennifer. This is so much fun."

"I'm sorry. It's getting late," she replied. Then she gave Stacy a pleading look with her eyes and it immediately registered with her, even in her drunken state.

"I'll get my coat," Stacy said.

Five minutes later, their car was being pulled up by a valet. They climbed in and drove away, heading toward the freeway. Stacy was out cold, sleeping in the passenger seat with her mouth open and a soft snore escaping from her mouth.

Jennifer dropped her drunk friend off at home, deciding that the kids could stay with her for the night. It would make the most sense. She also had to go into Stacy's purse to pay the babysitter, which was a slight jab to her financial state at that moment. Soon she'd get paid soon, though. Then everything would change.

With sleepy protests, the kids all loaded up in the car and made their way to Jennifer's house. Once at her home, they fell asleep quickly. After everything was organized, Jennifer went to bed too, but sleep eluded her a bit. She was thinking about the shock of her emotions that night, the annoying pushiness of that Gregory person, and also the way that George Sterling made her feel. There was something so familiar about him...mostly the expression in his eyes. She couldn't place it though and eventually she just chalked it up to a wild imagination.

The next morning, Jennifer was drinking some coffee in the kitchen, getting everything set for the kids to go to school, when the phone rang. It was Stacy.

"I'm sorry I fell asleep on you last night."

"It's okay," Jennifer said.

"How was I? I mean…was it bad?"

"No, you were fine."

"Good. And you, how are you?"

"Okay," Jennifer answered.

"I want to come over and help pack up the room."

"No, I got it."

"Should I get the kids for school?"

"No, I'll drop them off at school and then drop Clark off at home…or would you rather have me take him right to the babysitters?"

"Home. I need to see my baby before I go to work. I'll drop him off," Stacy said.

"Sounds good. I'll see you in a bit."

Jennifer hung up the phone and knew that Stacy was feeling guilty about the night before. She shouldn't. She had a lot going on and was like a pressure cooker. If she didn't let off the steam now and again, she usually exploded. And that was not a good thing.

Chapter Eighteen:
Elimination

Back from his little soiree to see Jennifer first hand, Tayyip was out of the painting and dealing with a very real, in the moment, issue. He was about to take care of the one person that he hadn't been able to persuade to enter his little competition of his own accord. It was too bad because part of the joy of watching the people that had ruined his life fall to the depths of hell was their willingness to participate. Nonetheless, he was eager.

Tayyip sat in his chair, facing the wall behind him. Pinned against that wall was no painting or piece of art; it was Dan Markel. His hands were spread out with nails tacked inside them. A rope was tied around his forehead in order to keep him focused straight ahead so he watch what was going on in the room. He couldn't escape looking at Tayyip. The look in Tayyip's eyes was delightful as he explained what was about to happen to him.

Without a shirt, it was easy to see Dan's strong muscles straining to pull his hands from the wall. From the corner of his eye, Dan could see a set of photographs also nailed to the wall. He tried to turn his head to see the pictures. One was a woman that has a red circle drawn around her face. The other photo was of a male that has been circled and crossed out with a red marker. He knew those faces, but he did not understand what was happening to him. He turned back to Tayyip, eyeing him up and trying to determine who he was and why he was so interested in him.

The curiosity, but lack of connection that showed on Dan's face interested Tayyip, reminding him that, to the Americans, his family was faceless and had no value. How else could he not recall him? He'd been particularly cruel to him, savoring in his wretched evilness. Tayyip stood up, walking over to him slowly. Each step was precise, showing that he had no fears or hesitation about what he was doing. He was calm and in control. If you could have measured Tayyip's heart rate at that moment, it would not have been escalated from the norm.

Enjoying the unfolding of Dan Markel's slow and painful deterioration, Tayyip casually reached for one of the long nails that was holding him up against the fine mahogany paneled wall and gave it a tap. Just the slight vibration of his tap made Dan wince. He clenched his jaw so he didn't give the man the satisfaction of yelling.

"Your toughness is impressive," Tayyip said. "Let's see what this does?"

Tayyip reached for a sharp medieval blade that was attached to a long wooden stick. It was sitting on the table just next to Dan; there to make him think about it and not allow curiosity about it to stray far from his thoughts. It had been effective. Occasionally he'd caught Dan straining his eyes to absorb its daunting impact from his peripheral vision. Swishing it through the air, Tayyip made it land just short of Dan's body, making the prisoner rapidly blink his eyes and then squeeze them shut, bracing himself for its impact.

"I will not do it yet. I wish to hear your pain," Tayyip said. He was smiling, but his words hissed out of his mouth like the sounds of a venomous snake.

"I won't give you the satisfaction. Why are you doing this?" Dan asked, staring at him directly, able to turn off his emotions in an instant.

"What? Do you think I have the wrong guy? Should I just let you go?" Tayyip's voice changed from a silky American intonation to one with a distinct foreign accent that Dan immediately recognized. His eyes went wide and then for the first time, a speckle of fear danced in them, bringing great satisfaction to his captor.

Dan began to plead now. "No, it can't be. You know it had been a mistake that day. I didn't know...none of us knew. Please don't do this."

"I recall saying those words to you and you not showing much compassion," Tayyip said. "Not only did I plead, but my Faridah also did. And then there was my son. You gave him no chance to beg or plead for anything as you watched him die."

"I'm sorry, I'm sorry," Dan said, tears starting to stream down his face.

"I'm sure you are now, but that hardly resolves anything," Tayyip said. He took the sharp medieval blade in his hand and swung it at Dan's neck. It severed his head, which did not fall to the ground, thanks to the ropes that still held it in place.

Tayyip walked over to the red-circled photo on the wall and swished a red X through it. He smiled, and then looked at the photo of the woman, Jennifer Koppell, and smiled again.

His men had silently been watching him in the corner, not saying anything or making their presence known until he requested it. Tayyip turned to one of them and said, "My Chinese Snake Fish are hungry. I think I'll feed them a little something." With that, he began to peel away small bits of flesh from Markel's body, strip by strip, and feed his 'babies.' All he had to do was turn to another painting on his wall, the one of the lake in which Jennifer was working, trying to figure out how the Chinese Snake Fish had appeared.

Chapter Nineteen:
Search and Seek

The FBI was swarming about, trying to piece together anything they could. Their field agents had confirmed that Shane Braff and his daughter were not at their home and that Jennifer Koppell, her daughter Amanda, nor anyone else in her family was at their home. Yet, they were watching them at their homes on the television screen. Was it some elaborate movie set? That hardly seemed possible.

Lead FBI agent: "Could they make one of those paintings so elaborate that it really portrayed a life? Nobody in Jennifer's story, including her, seems to realize they're in it. How could that happen?"

Agent Z: "Not sure. Braff certainly knows he's in his story."

Lead FBI agent: "And what's the word on Markel?"

Agent O: "Nobody can find him. Last sighting of him was this morning. He didn't show up for work and nobody has a clue where he is."

Lead FBI agent: "Keep looking for him and for Jennifer Koppell, her sister-in-law, or anyone else that can find her."

Agent Z: "We did get a confirmation that she went to Rhode Island with her entire family just two days ago. Same thing for Braff. The tickets were purchased through an agent and don't have a trail back to the person who paid for them, but they spared no expense."

Agent O: "They wanted to impress and they did a good job."

Lead FBI agent: "What about Markel? Did he have anything like that?"

Agent Z: "No, but he lives in Maryland, only six hours away, so he wouldn't have needed to fly."

Lead FBI agent: "We need to locate their families, parents, spouses, anyone they're connected to. They are all clearly in danger from the looks of it."

Agent O: "That's the weird thing about it, sir. They were all kind of loners after what happened with Nafisi that day. Their loved ones have either died or severed their ties to them. Everyone of meaning seems to be with them already."

Lead FBI agent: "Damn it! Okay, everyone, keep looking. We'll keep trying to stop this jam of the airwaves and find the physical location of Tayyip Nafisi. How's the trace going on him?"

Agent Z: "We keep thinking we have something, but then it leads to nothing. I don't know how a civilian can scramble signals like that, but they are doing a good job."

Lead FBI agent: "Don't mistake Tayyip Nafisi for a civilian. That's a huge mistake. He is one of the smartest men who has ever worked for us and his abilities exceed most. He's as dangerous and sharp a man as you'll ever meet."

Agent O: "And because he feels that the US really screwed him over, he's out with a vengeance, huh?"

Lead FBI agent: "The US and therefore, all Americans. It's one and the same to him."

Agent O: "Got it, sir."

Lead FBI agent: "Updates on the half hour please."

Chapter Twenty:
Boom

It was as if Tayyip Nafisi knew he didn't have as much attention as he'd wanted to have. His employees that were out and about in various bars, watching everything unfold had easily grown distracted with the interruption. They turned to conversations with each other, or simply diving into their smart phones and drifting away into their own thoughts. Americans were so shallow, from his point of view. It made it easier to understand how they hadn't become irate about what happened to him, but, then again, they'd done their best to cover it up and forget it happened so perhaps most didn't know. Ignorance was no excuse.

With a thoughtful smile on his face, Tayyip called one of his producers and told him what he wanted to have happen. He leaned back in his leather chair and turned the television up, enjoying a bottle of Perrier.

Suddenly, the television screen showed the desert. A loud fiery explosion rattled through the televisions and into every establishment or household that had them on. Yes, that would get their attention.

Shane carried Emily into the house and sat her down in a soft chair by an unlit fireplace. He looked around and saw a canteen in the corner, hanging on a peg. He quickly grabbed it and filled it from a bucket of water, tasting it first and then putting some of it on Emily's dried and parched lips. She groaned, asking for more.

"Slowly kiddo. You don't want to get sick again."

She nodded her head and drifted off to sleep. Shane just watched her, wondering what he'd done, allowing far too many demons from the past to infiltrate his mind. He finally snapped out of it when he remembered what Emily had said about the painting maybe knowing how to respond to them or evoke certain responses from within them. He'd been reluctant to admit it, but the thought had crossed his mind more than once now, which meant it had some validity to it.

Shane must have drifted off because he awoke to Emily grabbing her shirt, clutching it tightly. "It's so cold in here," she said.

It was cold. The temperature must have gone down forty degrees since he had dozed off. Shane looked around for some wood, but found nothing. "You wait here," he told Emily.

She waited, staring at a 3D image that was hanging on the wall, showing a video of a similar area. Suddenly, her stomach cramped, forcing her to find somewhere to vomit. She ran over to a nearby basket and leaned down, emptying what was left of her stomach. She collapsed on the floor, sweating profusely, yet so cold her lips were turning blue.

Shane found a blanket and went back to Emily. That's when he saw her on the floor and ran over, carrying her into the bedroom he'd found.

"Lift your head up, Em." She did so, barely having enough energy.

Emily whispered. "I'm sorry, Daddy. I'm sorry I let you down."

"Don't say that. I know they must have some kind of antidote around here somewhere. I need to find it and everything will be okay."

Shane left the room and Emily watched another television screen, staring at it with her gaunt eyes, which had large circles underneath them. Her breathing became abnormal and the cramping continued, but there was nothing left in her to come out. She had to deal with the misery of the situation.

It was dark outside by the time Shane came back, but he had managed to get some fire wood. He started a fire in the living room and carried Emily over to it. There had been some matches in the house. He put them into his bag, knowing they would be good to have. Once she was on a makeshift bed on the floor, looking at another one of the television screens, which continued to capture her attention, Shane went to get some things prepared. He came back in and sat down.

Emily said, "Is that you, Daddy?"

Shane stared at the screen, and then looked down at the floor. He was frozen, unable to talk. It was showing a pre-recorded tape of Tayyip Nafisi's house.

"Papa!" a small boy screamed. He ran over to his

father and tried to shove the soldier away. "Leave him alone!"

The response was a jab in the chest with the butt of the gun that sent the young boy flying backward. Nobody dared move to come to the boy's rescue for fear of their own lives. Another one of the soldiers turned to Tayyip and punched him in the face, sending his body flopping down to the side from the impact of the punch. Flecks of bright red blood splattered the soldier's hand. He sneered as everyone looked horrified, terror showing in their eyes.

Faridah Nafisi was pleading. "We are American!" Her voice echoed throughout the room like a loud speaker quaking the house inside.

Shane was horrified, staring at his daughter, who was not moving or even looking at him any longer. He'd had this dream before, of Emily seeing the most horrific thing from his past, aside from her mother's death, and now it was really happening. Then he noticed a green laser and suddenly the room when dark. All he could see were green lasers everywhere. He looked back at the fire and noticed a clock behind the logs ticking and a small digital clock was visible. He shouted, "We have to get out of here now!"

He was lunging for Emily, but she wouldn't wake. He looked closely at the design of the green lasers that were in the area before lifting up the rug. There was a latch that opened up, revealing a hidden room. He put Emily over his shoulder and climbed down the ladder, closing the door shut behind him. After what seemed like hours had passed, he slowly lifted the latch again and saw bright sun beaming in through the house windows. All was still. Then there was a loud explosion and the entire house burst into flames, causing Shane to cover Emily's fragile body in the furthest corner of the secret room, not knowing if the ceiling was going to cave in on them.

On the television, through the thick smoke, Shane Braff's face appeared. It was charred and his eyes were dilated; his hands over his ears, trying to quiet the deafening ring that wouldn't leave.

He stood with his daughter in a small narrow room, looking around, clearly interested. They'd managed to get down into the room when they realized that there was going to be an explosion and, once again, Tayyip was impressed with Shane's instincts, grateful that he was making his elaborate plan more entertaining. Word from his 'associates' was positive too, confirming that now everyone was watching everything unfold. They had all instantly believed that he'd died, along with his daughter. Now they had something to watch…something to root for…and eventually something to cry over when all was said and done.

There were many boxes in the room Shane and Emily found themselves in. Each the same size and square shape, stacked against the walls of the room. Shane walked over to them, trying to determine what may be in them. He pressed his ear against them, hoping to hear something, but he couldn't. His ears were still ringing from the explosion – a brilliant side effect that Tayyip hadn't planned for.

Little Emily was in the corner of the room, sitting there and still looking pale. However, her curiosity was piqued by all the boxes and she tried to get up.

"Stay there, kiddo. You need to rest while I figure this out."

She started to protest, but her weakness stopped her from giving too great an effort.

Shane began moving the boxes out of the way and some fell to the floor. He opened one up and jumped back briefly. Then he proceeded forward again with caution. The boxes were filled with grenades. There were so many of them. A rifle hung on the wall behind the toppled boxes.

"Why give me ammunition now?" Shane asked out loud. Then he thought better about questioning it and began to take as many as he possibly could.

"What Daddy?" Emily whispered.

"Just talking aloud," Shane said. He looked at her and didn't want to startle her by admitting that her words sounded like she was talking under water.

After moving some more boxes, Shane noticed that there was also a handled door in the wall, nearly hidden in the painting. That was where he needed to go because going back up wasn't an option. It must be the portal to a new painting, but what could he expect to find in the next painting? He knew he could handle whatever came his way, but Emily was a different story. She was still very sick.

Chapter Twenty-One:
Goodbye and Hello

Back home from taking the kids to school and dropping off little Clark, Jennifer walked into Issac's study, not ready to go to work yet. Nobody monitored her hours and she'd been putting in a lot of time so being a few hours late wouldn't be a big deal.

Once in the study, she closed the door softly and stared at the wall, examining the room with the large picture of Issac. She was gripping her coffee mug so tightly that her knuckles were turning white. Finally, she sat down at the black leather seat by the desk. It reclined back, making her smile. Issac always sat in that chair and she on his lap back when...

He'd tell her how beautiful she was, making her smile. Her hair was always tousled and she usually wore her favorite jeans and a t-shirt around the house. They'd kiss and talk about all the exciting things they had to look forward to; especially when their obligation to serve was done. Now she only had the memories. They kept her reliving the past, fearing the present, and not having the strength to think about the future. She'd become a prisoner of her own thoughts and her personal demons.

Something was poking Jennifer's side. She slid her hand into her pocket and pulled out the latest mortgage delinquency notice. It told her to pay $18,415.29 immediately to keep the house. As if the yellow copy on the house hadn't been enough of a reminder. She rolled her eyes, knowing that she had a huge uphill battle to come up with that type of money. Unless the government miraculously got their act together and paid her the benefits due, it wasn't going to happen. Then she remembered how the government's computers told them she was dead. Perhaps that's what they wanted. She couldn't deny that she'd longed for that on an occasion or two.

Her cell phone vibrated and she pulled it out of her other pocket. She looked at the number, but she didn't recognize it. She almost sent it to voicemail. At the last second she changed her mind, hoping it wasn't a debt collector.

"Hello," Jennifer said.

"Hello Jennifer. It's me, Gregory. We met at the party the other night."

Jennifer had an immediate desire to press the *end call* button. What did this guy want? "Yes, how are you doing?" She made sure her voice was cold and distant, not inviting.

Not wanting to talk to another man in Issac's office, she also walked into the kitchen, where she sat back down.

"I was hoping you could meet me for dinner."

"Oh, no thanks, Gregory."

"I didn't mean tonight. I meant sometime in the evening tomorrow."

"No thanks," she repeated.

"I wanted to talk to you about a job. There's an opening coming up in the firm and I think you would be perfect for it."

"I'm not sure what Stacy told you, but I have a job right now. I am already working."

Gregory insisted. "At least hear me out. It'll give you a little break and allow you to hear about something that may interest you."

A small battle between stubborn pride and seeking out an opportunity that may be better for her ensued. Jennifer knew she would be foolish to turn down an opportunity to listen, even if he was an obnoxious and pushy man. And, if she were to be completely honest, snake-fish were certainly not her passion. "Okay, sounds good." She couldn't believe she was saying the words as they came out of her mouth.

Jennifer hung up, went back to Issac's office, and suddenly packed everything as quickly as she could. She didn't think she'd have the courage to do it slowly. She just wanted to get it done before any more memories could invade her thoughts and stop her from finally getting it done.

As she packed up box after box, she could barely breathe, but she did it. As soon as she was done, she called Stacy to tell her she'd done it and about the call from Gregory.

Then she went to work, deciding to get home early and feeling entirely too unsettled about how her day had started out. It was the combination of everything more than any one thing in particular.

By the time she got home, she was surprised to see Stacy at her house, along with Clark and Christy. Jennifer looked at Stacy curiously and she mouthed, "He's packing some things." The former soldier nodded her head, knowing that the attempt at reconciliation must definitely be over.

After setting her purse and keys down, Jennifer went to the mailbox, carrying her daily glimmer of optimism that a check, the answer to all her prayers, would be in the mail. *Just one more week until you get paid,* she reminded herself.

Her hunch was wrong…again. There was nothing she wanted to see in her mailbox. She set the mail down on the counter and sighed, plopping it over the final notice about the foreclosure.

Amanda had been outside, planting something in the dirt, and came running into the house for a drink of water.

"Hi Mom. You're early," she said. She leaned in and kissed her cheek.

"And you're a mess," Jennifer said. She looked at her daughter in her blue soccer shorts, long white socks, and a v-neck sleeved t-shirt. She was no longer a little girl, despite Jennifer desperately clinging onto it. Certain days she wanted her to be a little adult, but on others, she just wanted to hold her close without her rebelling.

Amanda softly bit her lower lip and she looked at her mom. She clearly had something to say.

"What is it?" Jennifer asked, noticing her mannerisms.

"Mom, do you have some extra money to sign me up for baseball this season?"

Jennifer shook her head no. "Mom?" Amanda asked again, not seeing the shake of her mother's head. Honestly, she'd grown used to her mom getting distracted and often had to repeat herself.

Jennifer said, "Sorry. No honey, you will have to wait until next year."

Amanda wanted to complain about it, but she didn't. She understood how hard times were for her mom and, if she had the money, she'd let her play. It was so disappointing, but sometimes she felt like the kids whose parents were divorced. That wasn't the case with her though. Her dad had been a hero and he'd died during active duty.

Chapter Twenty-Two:
The Weakness

Something disturbed Tayyip as he watched Jennifer Koppell. She was so beautiful, yet so lost. The look of confusion in her eyes was genuine; the aching in her heart could be seen in everything she did. To most, she seemed a confident and competent individual, but he saw right through it. He wasn't pleased that her torment touched his heart, made him reconsider what he was doing.

He paced the floor, trying to process his unexpected emotions. It was absolutely unacceptable. Eventually, he poured himself a glass of Maker's Mark from his crystal decanter and drank it down, feeling its warmth trickle down his throat. Tayyip sat down in his chair, not interested in what was happening in his 'reality show' at that moment.

With his head back and in an unusually vulnerable state, Tayyip pondered everything. He's spent a great deal of time planning this out and finessing the technology. Yes, he was going to make billions of dollars by selling it to every enemy of the United States after this, but still... what was next for him?

Staring at his immaculate desk, Tayyip ran his hand across the top, removing a speck of dust he'd seen. His hand accidentally slid his desk pad a tiny bit. Something stuck out from underneath the pad. He pulled it out and stared at it.

Tears came to in his eyes as he looked at the picture of a once happy family. Faridah was standing gracefully, dressed in her colorful garbs for a family wedding, Hossien was smiling brightly, wearing a pressed white shirt and a black tie, looking like a proud young man. As for Tayyip, he looked at a version of himself that was as much of a ghost as what his wife and son now were. He could never be that man again – the man who was positive, loved what he did, and tried to make a good contribution to the world. The reality was that every person had a monster hidden within them. He just hadn't realized it until he'd been stripped down to a shell of a man, someone with no respect in the world he'd always tried to respect.

Staring straight ahead, unable to look at the picture any longer, Tayyip took his crystal tumbler that was filled with Maker's Mark and threw it against the wooden walls of his office. It made a loud thud before falling to the ground, not even breaking.

There was a knock on his office door and a voice called out, "Is everything okay, sir?"

"Yes," Tayyip called out. "Leave me be."

His order was their command and there was no other questions asked from the other side of the door. Tayyip stood up and walked over to a mirror he kept in the corner, and said, "I will never let such a moment of weakness happen again. Of this you can be sure, my loves."

Chapter Twenty-Three:
Desperation

Shane knelt down to help Emily get on his back. He stood up, making his way toward the door. Slowly turning the knob, he pushed the door open. They were standing in a very narrow tunnel. Unfortunately, the ceiling of the tunnel was very low. There was no other choice for Emily, weak and fragile, aside from walking.

Gently taking her hand, Shane led his daughter through the tunnel as quickly as he could without completely exhausting her. They had to reach that light at the other end of the tunnel. Hopefully, the antidote could be found in the next land. He had no idea what it was or even what to look for, but he was good at scouting out clues. Whoever the twisted fuck was behind this game was, they wanted to keep the hopes of survival alive...for now.

Suddenly the view was distorted and both the width and length of the tunnel stretched. Shane noticed glass. He reached out to touch it, but found himself stuck to it. When he pulled away, he started bleeding. It had nearly ripped the skin off his fingertips.

"Don't touch it, Emily," he turned around and warned. She nodded, barely holding on to his hand any longer, but she kept fighting through it, showing that she was not going to disappoint her father further or give up.

Without warning, the tunnel changed shape again, causing Shane to lay flat on his back and have Emily on top of him. He pushed backward with his legs, trying to move toward the end of it, but there were challenges along the way. The space was suffocating and it kept changing shapes, making it hard to move efficiently, and sometimes effectively.

Finally, an open field was within reach. Both Shane and Emily could see the trees swaying in the distance and the sun shining. They gave all they had to get out of that tunnel and eventually succeeded, ending up in an open dirt field.

The two stood up and stretched out their stiff and scraped bodies. Emily's frail finger pointed in the distance and Shane looked. There was a large rollercoaster standing tall against the sky. The brightly painted blue and white seats were easy to see. It looked inviting and fun, which was absolute torture. There was nothing fun about what they'd endured and likely had to continue enduring. It was evil and the idea somewhat sick and twisted.

Emily took a step forward and stumbled, falling down on her knees. Shane leaned down to see if she was okay and she nodded, but he could see how hard his angel was fighting back the tears. She still looked horrible and was in need of medical attention that far exceeded anything Shane could do at the moment.

He stood up and stared into the sky, not knowing if it was a painting, a television screen, or what. "Let her go! You want me. She has nothing to do with this." The look on his face was so genuine, so vulnerable. He was expressing his anguish and he could only hope for a bit of compassion in return. When he got out of this painting, he was going to kick some ass and get to Mathew Lengyel and whoever else was responsible for this. They had blatantly lied to Em and him, putting her in a dangerous situation. However, the voice in the back of his mind reminded him that he was the parent and he'd had the final say. His efforts to protect his daughter had once again failed, making a horrible situation grow even darker in his mind.

"Em, I'm so sorry I've failed you. I'm going to get us through this. You just hold on, okay kiddo?"

"Yes Daddy."

He looked down at her legs, They were all bruised up, more than they should have been, but the scratch from the tiger was gone. He should have been thankful for that, but he wasn't. It meant that he had less control over everything than he'd initially expected.

Shane slid off her socks and shoes to find her feet were also a bluish-purple, matching the color around her eyes. Seemingly before his very eyes, her hands also started to turn colors. It seemed like special effects from a movie, but it was really happening.

"Think," Shane ordered to himself. He moved into the field and looked around at the scenery. There was silence. He thought about himself for the first time. He looked at his daughter and their situation, knowing he must win it. He saw a wood post in the distance, straining his eyes to see it better. Balanced on top, a small silver tin can sat on a bucket. He smiled and lifted Emily up, kissing her forehead tenderly. "I need you to hold on."

Emily said, "Daddy." before she drifted off to sleep again.

Shane made it to the wood post. Its contents looked enticing. He lifted it up and found a syringe with a note that read: inject at your own risk.

Emily was clearly slipping away and he had to do something. He looked up at the rollercoaster, knowing it had some significance. But what? Then he saw it. There was something on the seat of the one at its highest peak. He lifted Emily's arm and checked her pulse before leaning close to listen to her breathing. It had become shallower than it was back at that house. It sounded like her lungs were filled with fluid and she was drowning. Was it really happening or was it the effects of that blast on his ears? Then he looked down at Emily's legs. He saw the bruises were getting darker and bigger too. His eyes kept drifting back to the syringe, debating what his best option was.

Shane took off running toward the rollercoaster with his daughter in his arms. When he got to the base of it, he set her down gently, and began scaling it. On the way to the top, he came across a bottle of water, which was good, but he needed more than water. He kept climbing toward the top. In the car at the highest peak, he found a brown bag with a bottle of pills inside of it. The bottle noted: take three times a day. There were ten pills inside. Shane moved out of the car, put the pills in his pocket, and began climbing down as quickly as possible.

Emily was lying there motionless. He opened the water, once again tasting it first. He helped Emily sit up, telling her she needed to find the energy to swallow some pills.

She was still very quiet and lifeless. He shook her until she woke up . She swallowed the pills and sipped a bit of the water.

Knowing that they couldn't stay still for long, Shane carried Emily to another spot at the base of the rollercoaster where he could see better. He found a strange lever sticking out of the ground. When he pulled the lever up, lights came on, blinking on and off, and carnival music began to sound out. It seemed so lively, yet the music echoed off the fields and woods in the distance, making it so eerie. He wouldn't have been shocked if some crazy looking clown popped out of nowhere at that moment.

Feeling like he didn't want to draw attention, Shane turned off the music and sat down on the dirt ground, resting his back against a steel girder that supported the ride. He picked Emily up, put her into his arms and stared out into the distance, not sure what to do. The sun began to set. He stared at its beautiful colors, wishing he'd taken time to appreciate them more in the past. Then he looked down at Emily and smiled. Her breathing was becoming regular. What he didn't realize was that the scene behind him was quite different, showing no signs of tranquility and calmness.

Chapter Twenty-Four:
Taking Time

Stacy stood in her office, wearing a black skirt and blazer to match her black pumps and white collared shirt. She was handling some papers and folders, writing busily at a table. The only other person in the room was a man in a stiff starched suit, sitting behind the desk, staring at a computer.

Mr. Keller said, "I need those on my desk by the end of the week. No excuses."

"Since when do I make excuses," Stacy began. She reminded him that she was finishing the report he'd asked her to do immediately. "This is going to take me the rest of the week. I think you should hand it over to Jim. He'd do a good job on it."

"I don't need good. I need great. You always work the fastest and most accurately. I can't afford to lose this client."

"How long have I been working for you?" Stacy asked.

"Ten and..."

She finished, "....and a half years. Yes, I know I am fast and efficient, but there are other people that do a very good job for the firm. Now is not the time for you to overload me with work. I have issues that I need to deal with at home."

Mr. Keller said, "I gave you time when you had your son. There is always something coming up at home and there will always be something at home, Mrs. Fave. *This* is important; the most important."

Stacy said, "I need to leave the office at 3:00 every day this week and next week so I can pick up my child from school."

"That's not acceptable."

"Then you are going to have to start looking for a new employee because it's non-negotiable," Stacy said, crossing her arms. She'd stopped working and was staring at Mr. Keller, showing she meant what she had said.

"This week and part of next week – that's it. Work your problems out on your own time. Unless they make the company money, I'm not interested."

Stacy said, "Thank you." She walked out the door, not looking back for fear of Mr. Keller seeing the pissed off glare she was sporting. That was the problem with these corporate law environments. Everyone thought their own crap was the most important thing in the world. These lawyers forgot that their employees were people with lives outside of work. Not everyone wanted to be married to their career. The thought made Stacy grunt, thinking of how she was technically married to Dave, but not emotionally. Honestly, her entire life was her kids, Jennifer, and Amanda.

Meanwhile, Jennifer was having her own struggles. She was at the El Paso biological lab. There was something she wasn't understanding. She didn't want to lose her focus, though. It was Friday and she'd have the weekend off. Staring at the data on her computer, she carefully handled the DNA sample of the Chinese Snake Fish. She moved slowly and methodically, placing a tissue sample under the microscope in front of her. Her head was down, focused on the matter on the small plate. She zoomed in on it.

Behind her, the snake-fish swam about the tank, showing their naturally aggressive nature. She'd finally gotten used to the noise, blocking it out so she didn't get jumpy. They seemed to naturally gravitate toward the glass of the tanks, smashing into it, and making everything jar as if they'd caused a minor earthquake. At first she'd thought it might be the glare, but she adjusted the lab to non-glare bulbs and put linings in the back of the tanks that would absorb light. It hadn't helped at all. Regardless of what she experimented with, they thrashed about, making it so she heard the noise in her mind at home.

Wanting to figure things out badly, the only thing that snapped her out of her work was her cell phone ringing. It was Stacy's ring tone and she reached over. "Yeah?"

Stacy said, "Are you coming home soon?" She had her on speaker phone. "Or are you working late again tonight?"

"I'm leaving in a half hour tops," Jennifer said.

"Okay," Stacy said. She didn't know why she was so anxious, but she was. She'd really had a lousy day.

Eventually, Jennifer did get home and Stacy left. Unfortunately for Stacy, when she got back to her house, all she felt was loneliness. Even knowing it would sting, she opened up the dark yellow folder that a private detective had delivered to her weeks ago. She'd kept it sealed, hidden in her bedroom closet. She had hoped that all would be well and she'd feel the love she used to have for him again. Well, it hadn't worked. It was time to open it up and see what she was up against. Maybe it would help her find the courage to take the steps toward true emotional detachment that she knew she must. She'd mentioned that she hated him, but truthfully, she just wanted to make sure she stopped loving him. That was her primary goal; her means of self preservation.

She walked to the kitchen and opened it up. Photos of her husband with a sexy younger woman were in front of her. They were being intimate and he showed such intensity – something he'd never shown her, even when they were first together. She swallowed hard, finally breaking into the tears that she'd tried to keep away for so long.

Stacy picked up the phone and dialed Jennifer up. "Hi."

"You okay?" Jennifer asked.

"No."

"We'll come over."

"No, we'll come over to your house. I don't want to be here. I'll get Clark and Christy set and we'll be there shortly."

Inside Jennifer's house, Christy and Amanda talked about snakes, thinking they could find some behind the fridge. Jennifer chuckled, wishing she could find the same enthusiasm for them. She'd never liked them and now, with the Chinese Snake Fish, she actually despised them greatly.

"I know you spend a lot of time worrying about me, but I've got to tell you...I am worried about you," Jennifer said, looking at Stacy. She had such sadness in her eyes, such a forlorn look.

"I'm alright. It's just hard. It's really time to move on." She breathed in and held her breath temporarily. "I can't believe I just said that so willingly. Yes, it is time to move on."

"Well, you know I'm there for you," Jennifer said. "Whatever you need help with, we'll figure it out together."

"Thanks," Stacy said, fronting a brave smile.

"I forgot to tell you. Guess who called me yesterday?"

"Who?"

"Your co-worker, Gregory."

"Oh yeah? Lots of women at the office would love to be in your position."

"Well, it wasn't for a date. He said something about having a job offer that I may be perfect for. He wanted to meet me today, but that's not going to work. I'll follow-up sometime next week."

"What? No way. Why are you still sitting here? Call him. Then get ready and go. I'll watch the kids so don't even try to weasel out with that excuse."

"I don't know. I don't want to meet him, I guess. What do you think about him?"

"Oh, don't ask me. I'm kind of done with men. I do know that he got Francine a good job. She's making good money. You need to get out more – don't let yourself be so tied down to grief."

"You know, you're the best sister-in-law any one could have," Jennifer said, smiling softly.

"I feel like I am more than that. You're my closest friend."

Jennifer smiled, sharing the exact same sentiment.

"Now call." Stacy slid Jennifer's cell phone in front of her and stared at her, not letting her off the hook.

An hour and a half later, Jennifer was at a restaurant with Gregory. He smiled at her as she walked up. "You look amazing."

"Thanks. I'm pleased to be here. I appreciate the invitation."

"No need to sound so formal," Gregory said.

"Sorry, just a bit nervous, I guess."

"Well, don't be. I'm pretty easy going and easy to talk with, so people tell me. So…tell me a little bit about yourself."

Jennifer laughed. It was an odd start to a job opportunity, one that felt more like a date, which scared her. "I work for the government and I have a daughter. My husband died in active duty…about three years ago."

Gregory looked at her and directly asked. "You ever thought about filling the void?"

"Excuse me," Jennifer began. "Void?"

"The void of not having a man around."

"Not your business. Look, all these questions about my personal life are putting me off. I'd rather relax, enjoy the evening, and hear about the job you'd mentioned. That's why I am here."

Gregory sipped his wine and stared at Jennifer. He moved closer, leaned in to her ample chest, and blew at her cleavage. She was shocked. He looked up at her and simply said, "Nice."

"Don't do that again," she said in a controlled voice. It was hard to believe that any man with good manners and an ounce of self-respect would do such a thing to a woman in public. What if someone had seen?

Gregory ignored her and turned to the waiter to motion him over. When he came he said, "Please bring us a bottle of your best whiskey."

"I don't drink whiskey."

"What would you like?"

"A glass of wine will be fine. I have to drive home."

"Bring us a bottle of white Cakebread. It's magnificent." The waiter nodded and left. Gregory turned back to her. "Have no worries. You are with me tonight. Order whatever you like and I'll take care of it. Enjoy."

"Thank you, but I am not hungry."

"You know, I was wondering if you could come back to my place tonight."

Thankfully Jennifer hadn't had a chance to take even a sip of water because she would have choked. "Excuse me?"

"You heard me. Don't play coy, Miss Koppell," he said, reaching his hand over to tickle the top of hers.

"I think it's time for me to go – to my place – alone," Jennifer said. She was shaken by the directness and nerve of this guy. He must have really thought he was something or that she was desperate, in some sort of rebound situation. He was wrong.

"No, you should stay and eat dinner. You won't regret it. It's not cheap you know."

Jennifer controlled her temper the best she could. "I couldn't have cared less if we were eating at McDonalds. Perhaps you should try to act like a gentlemen and stop with all the pressure and innuendos. Not only is it unattractive, it's also cliché and unoriginal."

"You know what? I am going to take your advice. Whatever the lady wants, the lady gets." Jennifer didn't get this guy at all. The bottle of wine came out and he filled his glass immediately, slamming it down and refilling it before she could even have a sip of hers.

A waiter came with their food a short time later and Jennifer sarcastically said, "It looks amazing." She began to eat, so frazzled she couldn't even enjoy the taste or savory smell.

After what seemed like hours, the meal was done and Jennifer was very aware that she'd been duped. He hadn't talked about any job opportunity a single time.

The waiter dropped off the check and Gregory reached into his suit jacket to pull out his wallet. Then he looked on the floor around him and announced, "My wallet is missing." The waiter heard his comment and began to look around the room as he waited on other tables.

"How is that possible?" Jennifer asked. Was this guy for real?

"I don't know how that is possible, but it's gone. Do you have it?" Gregory asked. He was looking at her like that was seriously a possibility.

"I've been nowhere near you. Just check again," Jennifer said, annoyed at the accusation.

He patted his suit jacket and pants again, repeating that it was missing until he had an audience of people watching him. They were looking at him like they thought he was a scammer. She half wondered if he was, too.

Finally the waiter came up and said, "Sir, are you ready to pay your ticket?"

"I don't have my wallet. How am I going to pay for it?" Gregory snapped.

"You and the lady may have to make some kind of arrangement, but this ticket has to be paid before you can leave this building or we'll have to call the police. Nobody wants that, sir."

"No shit," he snapped.

Jennifer took the check. It showed $200. Wow! That was a few weeks' worth of groceries for her and

Amanda. "Don't you frequent this place? Surely they know you," Jennifer offered.

"No, I don't and, obviously, they don't know who I am or I wouldn't be experiencing this ugly little encounter, would I?" Before Jennifer could tell him to take a hike, he asked, "Can you cover me?"

"I don't have that kind of money." Gregory stared at her in disbelief.

"Look, pay for it now. You know I'm good for it. I will make it up to you somehow."

"I told you, I don't have that kind of money."

"How much money do you have on you now?"

Jennifer said, "That's none of your business."

Gregory said, "Take care of this and I'll get to my bank right away in the morning and pay you back."

Jennifer felt so awkward. She slowly opened her purse, debating the situation. She had $250 in her wallet and she needed every bit of that to ensure that Amanda and she made it through the weekend without getting their phone and electricity cut off. She doubted they'd take a check from her either. Plus, when it bounced the cops would come looking for her anyway. This dinner had not even been her idea.

"Why don't you call a friend?" Jennifer offered.

"Are you serious? I am not doing that," Gregory spat.

"Well, why should I? This was your idea, not mine. You should have made sure you had your wallet before you left."

"Thanks for the advice," Gregory said.

Eventually Jennifer surrendered, taking out the money, only paying enough for the bill. Was it the waiters fault? No. She just added, "I'm sorry. This is all I have. He'll drop you off a very generous tip tomorrow when he pays me back."

Gregory was beat red at her snarky comment and she couldn't have been more pleased. In fact, it had been the highlight of her evening. She asked the waiter to cork the wine and box up the food. She was taking every bit of it with her.

Chapter Twenty-Five:
The Source

The agents were purposeful, but had a lead. Nobody was more surprised than they were to find out who the internal source for Tayyip Nafisi was; the one who had made it easy to hijack the television frequency and jam it.

Lead FBI agent: "Where's the station manager's office?"

Coordinator: "Down the hall. Why?"

The agent didn't respond to his question. He only spoke. "Take me to the office and unlock it if it's locked."

Coordinator: "I don't have the keys."

Lead FBI agent: "That's okay. I'm sure we can find a way to get in without them."

The agent nodded to Agent's O and Z, indicating that they should follow. The coordinator led them to the office door of Garret Vance, the station manager. They tried turning the knob; it was not locked. They went inside and began to rummage around the room.

Not sure where their rights lay and his job security ended, the coordinator could feel his nerves about ready to burst from his anxiety.

Coordinator: "Are you sure this is legal?"

Lead FBI agent: "You're not responsible. Don't worry. You can leave."

He didn't have to be asked twice. After the coordinator was gone, it didn't take long for the agents to find clues that the obviously clueless civilian had left behind.

Agent Z: "Look at this. A deposit receipt."

Agent O: "For how much?"

Agent Z: "A cool two million. That's a lot of money for a station manager to get."

Lead FBI agent: "Who wrote it?"

Agent Z: "It doesn't say on here, but I bet we can easily track it down. This guy clearly didn't think through what he was doing. Was lured in by the money."

Agent O: "Sending common sense out the window."

Lead FBI agent: "Same old story."

Within five minutes, they'd discovered that the check was drawn from a bank account in Newport, Rhode Island, with the name Paintings, Inc. on it. With a little further research, they discovered that Paintings, Inc. was owned by Tayyip Nafisi and had a location in Providence, Rhode Island. Acting CEO was a man known as Mathew Lengyel, who had now been traced to both Shane Braff and Jennifer Koppell. Things were getting interesting.

Lead FBI agent: "Let's get to Painting, Inc. headquarters immediately. I have a feeling we'll find what we really need to get into whatever the hell scene is unfolding on the television, save the victims and their families, and then secure the scene, and apprehend Nafisi. He can't be far away. He seemed to have a hand in everything. How many places can a man be in at once?"

Agent O: "More than most with this technology he's invented."

Within a half hour, the lead FBI agent, along with Agent's O and Z, were walking into Paintings, Inc. headquarters, along with twenty agents. They were ready for fast action and not going to mess around with anything. However, they were not expecting to find what they did in one of the first offices they entered.

A body was nailed to the wall, its flesh stripped off it in a slow, precise, and methodical manner. It was a gruesome sight, but none of the agents had time to dwell on how evil it was. If anything, it was evidence they had to get into the paintings quickly so they could save everyone that was trapped in them, knowingly or unknowingly.

As the agents swarmed around, the lead agent's cell phone rang.

Lead FBI agent: "Yeah...okay...be right there. And

oh…we found Markel – deceased."

He turned to his men and said they'd found the studios. Everyone working them had been secured and they needed to get there pronto to do the most bizarre rescue mission they'd ever had in their careers.

Chapter Twenty-Six:
Assault from the Woods

Shane had dozed off from exhaustion, despite his efforts to fight sleep. He had to remain alert and do everything he could to protect Emily. Feeling an intense light shining on his face, Shane was jolted awake. He put his arms up, trying to protect his eyes from the brightness before they finally adjusted. Once he could see again, he looked down at Emily lying with her head on his leg. He smiled, thankful that her bruises had started vanishing and her color was back to normal. He shook her gently, telling her it was time to take some more medicine.

She sat up and put the pill in her mouth, swallowing it down more easily than she had earlier. As she looked around, something in the distance caught her attention. She pointed at the strange object. Shane followed where her finger went. There was a post in the distance. It was holding a casket shaped box in the air.

"Do you think that's an entrance to a different painting?" Emily asked.

"I don't know. I'll check it out in a bit," Shane said. Before he could say anything else, the odd shaped box's lid lifted up. Shane looked around. He didn't see anyone and he wondered what could be in there. It was obviously something they wanted him to look at.

As if they sensed his hesitation, the contents of the

box began to float out of it, hovering in the air above it. He was surprised to see assault rifles, ammunition, a knife, and some other highly advanced military weapons. He would have loved to run to get those weapons because they'd likely be helpful, but he was also aware that he had an audience. In the bushes and woods that surrounded the weapons, men in their camouflage fatigues were staring at him, waiting for him to make a move. There were at least five of them and they all had guns and black war markings.

Shane turned to Emily, while keeping an eye on the men through his peripheral vision. She was staring at him curiously, but quietly. She knew her dad well and when he was focused or contemplating something, she stayed quiet. He winked at her before pulling down on the lever. The carts began to move up and Shane noticed something. They almost seemed to make a frame. He pulled the lever back down, stopping it.

"Emily, listen to me."

"Yes, Daddy," Emily said. She suddenly looked so scared. "I didn't think it would be like this. I don't know what's going on. I can't help you, Daddy."

"Don't worry, baby. You're going to be fine and I will be too. I need you to do something for me."

"What?"

"You need to scale up this rollercoaster and get to that black window up there on top. You can't worry about me. You have to make it through there. I know you're tired and exhausted, but you have to do it. Somehow you have to make it through there."

Emily said, "I'm not leaving you."

"I'll meet you at the other side. When you get there, be smart, be still, and don't talk to anyone. Got it?"

"But Daddy," Emily said, trying not to cry.

Shane paused, looking at his daughter and knowing that he was asking so much of her. This was a horror beyond anything that her ten year old frame of reference could imagine. "You can do it, kiddo." He kissed her head and turned around to survey the horizon for the men again. They'd all switched positions.

Emily stood up and began scaling the rollercoaster. As she got higher up, she didn't dare look down to see how far she'd gone. She stared up and it seemed so far away to the top. Her arms were weak, but she kept on going. She didn't want to disappoint her dad and she knew that he'd be there in a bit. Nothing or no one could beat him. Shane watched her, not wanting to move from that spot until he knew she made it safely through that window.

Gunshots started to echo across the field, making him turn away from Emily. He tried to assess where they were coming from, but they seemed to be coming out of nowhere. One of the bullets hit a steel post on the rollercoaster and Shane panicked. Were they trying to shoot Emily? He looked back up and saw that she was standing on the top cart of the rollercoaster, getting ready to dive through the black window.

"Hurry!" Shane shouted this as loud as he could, hoping it would be louder than all the gunfire that had begun to sound out.

He saw Emily go into the black window and breathed a sigh of relief. She was safe, but now he had to wipe out the threats to their continued safety. From what the rules had indicated, anything could go through those windows, but the window couldn't seal unless they were both through. That meant his plan was to keep the combatants away from the window until he could eliminate them and go through it himself. If they wanted an all out battle, they were going to get it. Nobody – absolutely nobody – was going to mess with his daughter again in The Land of Paintings.

Shane took off running, making his way toward the weapons. It felt like a fool's mission, but he knew he didn't stand a chance if he didn't get some sort of weapon. He saw a thick pile of wood near the box of weapons and began to run toward it, hoping he could get cover there.. As he sprinted across the field, gunshots fired on him, pounding into the dirt field, and sending out billows of dust into the horizon. The sky was still so bright, making it hard to see very well. Finally, he reached the wood pile. Every one of the bullets fired missed him. He knew the odds of that were highly improbable. This was real life, or at least it seemed it was, and he should have been laying face down in the field. For some reason, they didn't want him dead.

Not able to get to the weapons, Shane contemplated what to do next. He heard a noise from behind a bush about ten feet away from him. He could tell that a person wasn't there because it was thin enough that they couldn't possibly disguise themselves. However, he could see a silhouette of something. Someone had just put something there. What was it?

Knowing he had to make a run for it, Shane ran the ten feet to the bush, feeling bullets whizzing over his head, and dove behind it. Now he was really surprised. There was a pile of bricks and also five grenades. They were like the ones he'd tried to take from the odd tunnel, but had to abandon. He hadn't been able to safely transport them at the time. Now someone was giving him some to use. Interesting.

Picking one up and pulling out the pin, Shane tossed it into the woods in the direction that the firing had been coming from. He'd lost sight of the five men and was going on blind luck, hoping he'd hit someone or at least make the bastards retreat so he could get a weapon and get back to that rollercoaster.

There was silence in the woods. The gunfire stopped. Shane wasn't sure if he'd actually eliminated the problem or had caused them to retreat. Maybe neither. He began tossing the heavy red bricks into the woods, hoping to hear a grunt or groan if they connected with a person. They'd certainly hurt like hell. There was no response though. With no other options, he decided he had to pursue the weapons to see if anyone was there. If he had a gun, he could find a way to flush them out and take advantage of a clear target instead of hoping to hit something hidden in the woods.

Running to the box, he grabbed two guns and two belts of ammo. Shane stood behind the stump and filled his magazine quickly. That was one skill that had never left him from his days of service. He could get a gun loaded and locked in fifteen seconds flat. Every second was valuable.

The second the last bullet was in the magazine, the gunfire resumed. It seemed like bullets were flying at Shane from every direction. He turned in circles, firing back, but seeing nothing. The intensity was unreal. Shane felt the heat of the bullets, but saw no people. It was as if the air was rapid firing on him. Then he felt it. One of the bullets connected, piercing his thigh and sending him down to the ground in instant agony. It had hit a major vein and blood was spurting out everywhere, splattering his face and painting the dirt field red. Everything started to blur and dizziness instantly consumed him. Shane had just enough wits about him to take his belt off and squeeze it around his leg, cutting off the blood flow so he wouldn't bleed to death. Just as he buckled the belt, he couldn't take the pain or the shock any longer. His body slumped over, lying motionless in the field.

Chapter Twenty-Seven:
The Guests are Arriving

Tayyip was enjoying preparing his new temporary home for the activities that would take place shortly. Oh, how they'd all be surprised when it came together. Two people that feared him, pitted against each other, having to choose between those they loved and their own survival. There had never been a better television show. And it was all orchestrated by him.

There was a knock on the door. Tayyip raised his voice slightly, "Enter." He turned around, looking poised and polished in his khaki pants and red polo short.

"You must have an update for me," Tayyip said.

"Yes sir," Gregory Meskar said. He looked at his boss, hesitating for a moment.

"Well, what is it?" Tayyip asked. "Please just say it, Gregory."

"One of our guests has arrived," Gregory said.

"Really? Who is that?" he asked.

"Emily Braff, sir."

"Where's the father? He is alive, isn't he?"

"He is sir, but he's injured. He was crafty and sent her through the window without him."

"Ah...to make sure that he eliminated anyone that may try to follow them through. Very clever, I must admit."

"What shall I order now, sir?"

"Make sure he comes to and do whatever you must to make it challenging for him to get through that window. The second he does, close it up. Make sure he can see Emily right away when he's in this painting. And oh...make sure there's a little something shocking in between him and his daughter."

"Your favorite, sir?"

"Yes, my favorite would be perfect for this."

"Okay. Anything else?"

"No, you're excused, Gregory. Please make sure I keep getting updates. Sadly, I don't have time to watch my own masterpiece unfold. There is somewhere that I have to be soon."

Gregory left and Tayyip walked over to a drawer. He pulled out a wig and some other accessories. He smiled, running his fingers down the long brunette wig. What an adventure he was about to have.

Chapter Twenty-Eight:
A Woman Scorned

The pictures had been the last straw for Stacy, showing that David Fave was clearly not committed when it came to saving their relationship. Every second longer she accepted it, meant he was playing her for a fool. She would not accept it any longer, for her sake as well as her children's. They could go back to having every other weekend with their father since he was more interested in sticking it into someone else than spending time with them. If it was just Stacy, she might understand, but he'd turned his back on his children and that was unacceptable. What kind of man did that?

Standing in line at the bank, Stacy looked around with a gleam in her eyes. She was tapping her perfectly polished pink nails, eager to take care of her banking. In fact, she hadn't been more excited for something in a long while.

The bank clerk looked at her, "You know that if you withdraw this much, the account will be closed."

"Oh, I don't want that. Make sure you leave a dollar in there, or just enough to keep it open."

"You'll want enough to cover your monthly fees. They come out today, ma'am."

"That's fine then. When you get my money, make sure you give me all hundreds and a few extra rubber bands too."

"Planning a trip? Perhaps traveler's checks would be a wiser choice. That way you'd have insurance with them."

"Oh no, nothing like that. Just a little surprise for my husband."

"I see. Hopefully we have that many hundreds on hand, Mrs. Fave."

"As many as possible if you don't. You can do the rest in fifties, but only if necessary," Stacy said, smiling sweetly at the teller. He blushed at her flirtatious behavior. Little did he know that she wasn't flirting at all. She was feeling happy and liberated. Today was a great day.

Ten minutes later, the teller was back with the money. A manager stood next to him as he counted it. She stared down at all the money and then up to Stacy, not sure what to say. After it was all confirmed she smiled. She put the banded load of money, a little over forty thousand dollars, into her hand bag and made her way outside.

Twenty minutes later, she was heading toward the school to pick all the kids up. The window was down and she was enjoying the nice breeze that came with her El Paso day. When she saw Christy and Amanda coming, she stuck her arm out to wave to them.

"Hi Mom," Christy said.

"Hi dear, how was your day?"

"Pretty good. Glad school's done because Amanda and I want to play outside."

"And you, Amanda, have a good day?"

"Yeah, it was okay. I had a spelling test – yuck."

"Yuck, but necessary," Stacy said. As an afterthought she added, "It really is a fantastic day, isn't it?" Then she turned up the music and sang a song, which made Christy and Amanda snicker a bit. She wasn't known for being a great singer, although she loved to sing a lot.

Next, it was off to the daycare to get Clark. She was going to surprise everyone with Chinese for supper. It was going to be a fun evening. To heck with all the things that should be done, they were going to do what they wanted to do. Sure, Jennifer might fuss for a minute, but she'd get over it in awhile. Stacy was sure of it.

Jennifer pulled into her driveway just ahead of Stacy and the kids.

"Wow! What great timing," Stacy said. "You hungry? I picked us up some Chinese – all our favorites."

"Yum!" Jennifer had a weakness for Chinese food, like some people do for chocolate. She just loved every tantalizing taste of it. "What's the occasion?"

"Simply celebrating a beautiful day, hanging out with the people I love best," Stacy said.

Jennifer took her at face value. She probably was ready to diffuse a bit since David was definitely not going to be in her life any longer. She had been there herself, albeit under different circumstances.

The kids didn't waste a second. Jennifer got some plates and forks out to set the table and they all sat down. She paused to look at Stacy, watching her for a second. She couldn't tell what it was, but something was different. It was hard to pinpoint.

"Wow...you're looking amazing. What did you do?" Jennifer asked.

"I just bought a few things," Stacy replied, smiling brightly.

"Well whatever it is, it's awesome. I'd swear your skin is glowing. I could probably use some of that. I'm getting a farmer's tan from being on that boat the past few days."

She shrugged, knowing that David was on his way to the house to pack his remaining things and that it would be the end of him being in that house permanently. Their separation would soon turn into the divorce that they'd avoided for nearly three years. Although she didn't love her baby any less, it didn't escape her that it was a keen sting to have Clark as a result of a 'moment of passion' with David that could have been avoided. It had delayed the inevitable even longer. After David removed the rest of his things, his instructions were to leave his key on the counter. It was mostly symbolic, as she already had a locksmith coming in the morning.

After some great laughs and full bellies, Jennifer began to clean up the table. In the meantime, Stacy fed Clark.

"Thank you, Stacy. This was such a nice surprise. I had been prepared to eat the leftovers from my horrible night with that Greg. This is considerably better, especially the company."

"How odd that he was the way he was," Stacy began. "Doesn't seem that way at work; not according to all the ladies who pursue him at least. I guess you just never know what a man might do, huh?"

"Nope," Jennifer said. She couldn't help but notice that Stacy's blue eyes darkened a bit at the mention of a man doing something wrong. Jennifer had to remember that she was just beginning to start a journey that would have just as many rough days as blissful days.

Then there was a knock at the door, making any chance for further discussion disappear, at least for the moment. Jennifer paused, not feeling like answering it.

"Well, aren't you going to get that?"

"They'll go away," Jennifer said.

The knocking on the door got louder. Then the

doorbell started to ring. Jennifer was frozen, having a bad feeling about that door.

"Come on. They're obviously not going away," Stacy said.

Jennifer heard Amanda and Christy's voices. They were both upfront. "Yes, she's home," she heard Amanda say.

Now there was no choice aside from answering it. Jennifer ran toward the front door and swung it open. She stared at the man before turning to Amanda and Christy. "Why don't you two go out back and play some more, okay?"

"Okay Mom," Amanda said. The kids took off and Jennifer could turn her attention to the man on her front steps.

The man was wearing a black suit with a white shirt and gray tie. Very practical. He was very tall, but had kind eyes.

"Yes, how may I help you?"

"Jennifer Koppell?"

"Yes."

"I'm Otis Davenport, ma'am. I'm sorry to inform you, but you have been served." He extended his arm, holding out some papers and Jennifer grabbed them, her heart racing. What was this for?

"For what?" Her voice sounded cool and collected, but inside she was frantic, trying to determine what it might be.

"This is your eviction notice. They filed a claim with the police department. You need to sign this. It's a notice saying you have received your final eviction notice and you have to move out."

"What? Why would that be? I don't understand," Jennifer rambled. Question after question flowed from her mouth, trying to think as each one spilled forth.

"I just bring you the news."

Jennifer looked around. She saw a man sitting in a car at the edge of her driveway. "Is that the owner of the bank?"

Otis nodded. "He wanted to see for himself that you got it."

Jennifer said, "Oh really. Is that standard protocol?"

"Not my place to say, ma'am."

Jennifer hadn't known it, but Stacy had walked up behind her. She swung the door open and smiled at Otis. "Why don't you have the owner come in?"

"Stacy, no," Jennifer said, glaring at her. "I have this under control. I don't want him to come in."

Stacy ignored Jennifer, pushing past her friend. She looked at the owner and waved to him, beckoning him in. Surprisingly, he got out of the car and began walking toward the house. He had a confident gate and content gaze, acting as if throwing someone out of their home was no big deal.

"What are you doing?" Jennifer whispered to Stacy, yanking her back into the house. "We can't seduce him into forgetting about the papers he just served. Are you crazy?"

Then Stacy reached over, grabbing her hand bag. She pulled out wads of money, all rubber banded together. Jennifer's eyes almost popped out of their sockets. "Where did you get that?" Jennifer asked incredulously.

"I drew all of it out of the bank. I had the money transferred from our joint account to my savings account. I am saving some for any expenses I may incur and the rest is going to settle your debt. How much is it?"

"Does he know this?" Stacy asked, aware that Otis was staring at the two of them with interest, as well as the owner now, who was standing at his side.

"No he doesn't know. He is not taking all of our money with him. He has to start all over too." Stacey's eyes were determined as she put her hand on her hip. "Girl, come on. How much do you need to give to pay this debt in full?"

Jennifer couldn't answer, but the owner of the note did. "$18,415.29 plus an additional $500.00 for processing fees. That makes the total…"

"$18,915.29," Stacy replied, smiling at him. "Here's an even $19,000.00. Keep the change," she said.

"How can I ever thank you? I only have $400 to pay you now," Jennifer began.

"Don't worry about it, hon. I love you and am glad I can help. However, you can watch the kids tonight. I have a bag with all their things in the trunk."

"Absolutely," Jennifer said.

Stacy moved around the men to the car and clicked her key fob, popping open the trunk. She was back a minute later with two bags. "You going to be okay?"

Jennifer nodded yes. "Look, you don't have to worry. Just go. Everything will be fine here. And…thank you. I don't know what I would do without you." Jennifer hugged her tightly, feeling an overwhelming sense of relief come off her chest.

Stacy went to her car, leaving Jennifer face to face with the owner, but she was smiling. The game had changed.

"You can tear that letter up. It won't be necessary. Would you like to come in for some coffee?"

"No thank you, Ms. Koppell…or is it Mrs.?" The owner asked this question so calmly that it sent a chill down Jennifer's spine. She looked into his eyes. They seemed so familiar. She wondered where she'd seen them before. It seemed like it had been recently.

After he left, Jennifer paced around the house, feeling grateful and overwhelmed by what had just happened. Clark had fallen asleep so she sat at the table, figuring out how she could pay Stacy back when she got her first paycheck – which would be in three days time. Then, after she got the settlement, Stacy would be her first priority to pay in full.

Later that night, after all the kids were tucked in and sleeping, the adrenaline rush of Jennifer's day ended. She collapsed into bed, exhausted. She fell into a deep sleep and her dreams took over.

That night, she dreamt about the owner of the house note. As she stared at him, he suddenly turned to Stacy's boss, George Sterling. They looked so similar. Actually, no they didn't, except for their eyes.

Chapter Twenty-Nine:
Programming Interrupted

There was no time to hesitate or rethink the plan, the FBI agents had to get into those paintings. They had the staff of Tayyip Nafisi, who were frightened and singing like song birds to avoid prison time, helping them enter the painting. It had been determined that too many agents would not be wise so the two that were chosen to enter into the painting were Agents O and Z.

Agent O: "Ready, lower me down."

Agent Z: "Second that."

Lead FBI agent: "Okay, you're being lowered into The Snake, the painting they say that Emily Braff is currently in. Look for her, find her, and try to retrieve her. After that, we can search for Shane Braff and the others. Got it?"

Agent O: "Yes sir."

The ropes lowered the two agents down. Only they hadn't landed in the place they thought they would. They were in a dark room, looking like they were the fish in the tank instead of all the fish that were swimming at the glass around them.

Chapter Thirty:
Behind Closed Doors

Dave pulled up to the house, exhausted from a hell of a day and dreading moving the rest of his things that night. He hoped he'd be done before Stacy got home because he was in no mood to argue. Sure, he'd messed up, but he hadn't meant to hurt anyone. However, despite how little she thought he knew her, he could see how badly he'd hurt her. He knew that he'd never given her his all. She'd always given him her best.

The cell phone on his hip started to vibrate. He leaned down to check his caller ID. "Hi," he said solemnly, but there was a smile on his face. "Yes, I can, but now is not a good time," he said. His jaw tensed and he shoved his free hand in his pocket, pressing down firmly with it.

A second later he said, "I have to move fast and pack. I have no idea when she will be home and I know she just doesn't want to see me here...No, I don't want to see her either...No, it's not a good idea to come help...Look, I better get going. I'll just plan on seeing you tomorrow, okay?"

He tried to hang up but the voice on the other end kept talking. The more his conversation carried on, the more aggravated he got. He finally said, "There is no need for us to get together at this house." He hung up, trying to figure out what to do first. It wasn't easy. He looked around and, even though he was there alone, he could hear the kids' laughter and Stacy making her comments at the television as she watched those talk shows she enjoyed so much.

There was a knock at the door. Dave went to answer it. He stared coldly. "I told you it wasn't a good idea," he said. "Sorry, I just can't."

"Maybe I can get you to change your mind," Regina cooed, smiling at him in a wicked, seductive way.

David looked at his little brunette dish and her eager face. Her body was built for pleasure, which was enhanced by the revealing shirt and the tight pants. It made his temperature rise and his pants bulge.

She followed him to his office, where most of his important papers were kept. He began to organize things, trying to block out what his body wanted to do. Dave turned around and froze. Regina was stretched out on the table, showing her curvy presence to him. It was more than he could take at that moment. He longed for a release that only she could give. *What the hell*, he thought. *He liked a good gamble.*

Regina was naked, staring at him with some papers in one hand. She called him over seductively. Her breasts looked amazing. They bounced with the liveliness of a young woman, one whose body hadn't been changed by childbirth and the comfort that slipped in when she assumed her husband would only be faithful to her – that he'd never stray or act on his desires for someone else.

"This is what I wanted you to look over before we present the report to the board tomorrow. Someone screwed with the numbers. This is not what I reported," Regina said. Dave snatched the papers from her, looking at them with aggravation. He wanted to slide into her and take her for a ride, not deal with business.

"What? Let me see that. This is what couldn't wait?"

"Yes look," Regina said, purring like a kitten.

"You're distracting me, babe. Give me a minute," he said.

"And that is a bad thing?"

"It certainly doesn't look like a good thing," someone said. Dave whipped his head around to find Stacy standing there. She glanced casually but kept walking by.

Regina didn't do anything to change her pose, not caring if she'd walked by. Might make her life easier.

"Stacy! Stacy! It's not what you think," he shouted. Then he turned to Regina. "Get the hell out of here now."

Regina shrugged and slowly started getting dressed, taking her own sweet time. The smirk on her face gave it away that she thought it was amusing. She couldn't wait for him to explain everything to the soon-to-be ex about what she'd just seen.

She gathers her papers and nodded at Dave, who was pacing around and freaking out. "It's a pleasure doing business with you. I'll see you tomorrow, hon."

He walked Regina to the door, not talking the entire time. He held her arm tightly, like his fingers were a vice grip, until she was out the door. The he closed it quickly, locking it behind him.

He ran to find Stacy, who was in their bedroom. Dave tried to put his suave demeanor on, the one that had swooned Stacy when they'd first met. "Listen hon, there is something strange going on. That wasn't what you thought...I don't understand it, but..."

Stacy put her hand up to cut him off. "Yeah, you think?" Then she turned her back to him, putting the money into her safe while he was talking. Just like she'd hoped, it caught his attention.

"What are you doing?" Dave asked.

"Making sure I get everything I deserve."

"What's in the safe?"

"Your money. Well, my money now. I emptied our bank account."

"You did what!"

"I think you heard me. Why don't you have some wine, find one of your sluts, and relax. Chances of our divorce being amicable at all went out the window when

222

I saw what you invited into my home."

"You're talking crazy. Please listen to me. You didn't see what you thought you did," he said.

"A naked whore sprawled out on your office table. I'm pretty sure I saw that, David."

"Let me explain," he pleaded again.

"There is nothing you can say. Just get out," Stacy proclaimed.

"Not until you hear me out." He snatched her arm and held her tightly. She slapped him across the face with her free hand.

"Do not touch me. You have no right to place one of your filthy hands on me!" Stacy was trying to control her emotions so she didn't start crying. She couldn't give him the satisfaction of that.

"Honey, please. I love you more than anything in the world. I can't lose you. Not like this. I was here packing, trying to do what you asked, but then she called. I told her not to come over, but then she was there. I just turned around and she was undressed. Honest."

"You must think I'm pretty dumb. Just stop it, Dave. Stop it now! Finish packing and get the hell out. You're no longer welcome in this home or my life."

"You can't do this." He walked over to the safe and tried the old combination.

"It's been changed. I'm smarter than you. Always have been and I definitely wouldn't have been dumb enough to get caught fucking someone in my own home. You see that's the difference between us."

"What are you saying?"

"You figure it out." Stacy dashed back.

Stacy held her head down, wiping a tear out of her eye. She couldn't look at him. He eventually lifted his arms up in the air in surrender and headed toward the closet to get some suitcases to pack all his clothes.

He took some of his clothes from the hangers as quickly as possible, taking his frustrations out on his clothes. Then he grabbed a few pairs of shoes as a side thought and shoved them in the suitcase, closing it up.

He didn't say a word as he walked out of the bedroom into his office. He grabbed his files from his cabinet and put everything from his desk in a box, feeling like he was being fired from a job.

Stacy followed him to the front door when he was done. He was going to walk out without saying a word, but she had something she wanted to say to him. At the front door Stacy said, "Good luck finding your way now. Good luck finding another woman like me and good luck keeping your life together without me."

"It doesn't have to be this way."

"But it is this way. It is."

"I love you and I always will."

"Me and how many others?" Stacy asked. She didn't wait for an answer. She closed the door, feeling like she was going to explode. The last thing she wanted was to have Dave see her breakdown. She noticed him staring at her for one last second before he turned around to leave.

Stacy couldn't believe it. She went to the kitchen for a bottle of wine and made her way to her bedroom, lying down on the bed, prepared to drink her troubles away that evening. First, she cried. Then, she was angry. Then, she repeated the emotions all over again.

Suddenly, she heard a noise. She got pissed, thinking that Dave had tried to sneak back in. *What an asshole! Couldn't he leave bad enough alone*, she thought. *Selfish prick.* She listened for the source of the sound before going to the drawer in her night stand for the gun. It wasn't there. Dang it. Where had Dave put it? That's right...the bathroom.

She peeked out into the hallway and saw that the light was on in the bathroom. Someone was definitely in the house. Not having anything to defend herself with, Stacy snuck back into her bedroom and grabbed her spikiest pump. She was ready to gouge out the eye of anyone who lunged at her, or throw it at them with all her might.

Slowly walking down the hallway, she could feel the carpet beneath each foot. She realized it would have been a good idea to put on sneakers, in case she had to run like hell, but it was too late. She inched step by step to the bathroom door, slowly opening it up. No one was in there. She quickly shut the door and locked it behind her, pressing her ear against it. She didn't hear a sound.

Breathing in, Stacy felt like she was suffocating herself from the anxiety of the moment. She couldn't stand it and tried to calm herself. She wouldn't be able to do anything if she was so startled. She reached up to grab the gun from the small ornate box on the shelf.

Stacy slowly opened up the chamber and groaned. There were no bullets in the gun, nor were there any in the box. Where were they? What good was a gun for self defense if there was no ammunition for it? Then she looked to the side of the box and found a single bullet there. She reached for it with shaking hands and loaded it into the gun. Breathing in and thinking to herself that she could handle it, she slowly opened the bathroom door, ready to approach whoever might be in the house.

She didn't have to wait long. As soon as she was out in the hallway the closet door across from her slowly opened. She couldn't believe who she saw standing there. It was someone who was dressed just like her. It startled her enough that she didn't know how to respond.

This person was wearing a brunette wig cut and styled just like her hair, the same color lipstick and nail polish, even an outfit from her closet. The person looked like her, but wasn't her. They had different eyes.

Stacy pointed the gun and pulled back the hammer,

frazzled but not willing to ask questions before defending herself. The gun was on the imposter, but they were not threatened by it. They looked at themselves in a small compact, checking their lipstick. Then they set it down, still not paying attention to Stacy or the gun she was holding. Then they put on some cream colored leather gloves.

The impersonator looked at Stacy and began to talk. Her eyes widened when she heard the voice of a man, but she kept the gun steadily pointed at him.

"You know that it's Jennifer's fault. The reason your husband cheated, the reason you will die tonight, and the reason your children will grow up without a mother."

"Who are you? What are you talking about?" Stacy asked.

"Think about it. What has haunted your sister-in-law for so long?"

Stacy paused, trying to process his words. Then it came to her. "Tayyip Nafisi?" She questioned the possibility.

"Yes, you are smart; just like you told your husband earlier," he said.

Stacy began trembling again, trying to keep her emotions in check. "Please no."

"I have no choice," Tayyip said.

"You're not going to get away with this."

"Blame your brother."

"What?"

"Issac Rainnek is the one who took my family away so I am going to take his. His wife was there and she did nothing to stop them. She will pay for that. She, like you, will pay."

He thrust forward and startled Stacy. She screamed and the gun fired.

Chapter Thirty-One:
The Warrior Mentality

Shane woke up and could feel the dirt against his cheek. His leg ached so badly. Bolts of pain were going through him, making him feel sick to his stomach. He didn't want to move since he couldn't assess the scene properly, but he looked down toward his leg and saw that the blood that had been bright red was crusted over. That meant his wound was starting to heal. That was good. However, it was hard to tell who may be around him or what was going on in regards to the insane amount of gunfire that he'd just experienced...however long ago that was.

The sky was getting darker, but that didn't mean anything. It could change colors at will in the damn Land of Paintings. It took every bit of effort Shane had to sit up. The entire time his body was tense, not sure if he was going to get shot at again.

Now sitting, he used his arm to keep his body stable as he looked around to survey the scene. He didn't notice anyone around him. As a matter of fact, it was completely silent. Had they thought he'd died? He hoped so, but didn't want to assume it. Breathing in to control the pain and block it out of his mind, Shane stood up and looked around.

He saw the weapon he'd used a few feet away from him and he reached down to grab it, going as quickly as possible. It was slow though. He was stiff, sore, and still lightheaded from the loss of blood.

Looking in the distance, Shane saw the rollercoaster there, but he wasn't quite ready to head that way in case someone did follow him. It could be a trap. Instead, he walked the opposite direction of it, looking at the perimeter of the woods and listening for any noises that may indicate a human or animal presence. There was nothing.

Then a scratching noise came. Shane looked around, trying to figure out where it was coming from. He didn't see anything until his eyes fell upon the rollercoaster. It was slowly being erased before his very eyes.

Damn it. They'd wanted him to be untrusting. He couldn't go fast, but Shane started to run to the rollercoaster as fast as he could with his wounded leg. There were many dips in the field and he kept falling down, not able to maintain his balance while crossing them. When he didn't fall down, the sudden drop jarred his body so bad that he couldn't stop a tear from streaming out of his eye.

Each step became more urgent and Shane did everything within his mental ability to block out what was physically wrong with him. If he didn't get to the top of that rollercoaster in time he'd lose Emily forever. He couldn't allow that to happen.

Finally, he reached the rollercoaster. Nearly one half of it was already gone – vanished into thin air. He started to scale up the girders; thankful he could rely on his upper body strength and give his leg a bit of a rest. The wound had opened back up, making everything around him fuzzier.

"Focus!" He shouted. He started talking aloud like he was a drill sergeant, knowing it would get his adrenaline flowing and give him the energy he needed to make it to the top. He could see the black window but it was getting darker out. The window seemed to be moving ever so slightly every time he didn't look at it.

He was within ten feet of the top, almost to the window, when the gunfire started again. It sprayed all around him, ricocheting off the steel, making a deafening ringing in his ears. It was maddening. He wished he had something to cover his ears with. Anything at all would have been helpful. Yet, the shots kept missing him.

Finally making it to the edge of the window, Shane looked around one last time and saw nothing, but he could hear screams in the distance. "Daddy, Daddy!" It was Emily. He couldn't tell if they were coming from the painting he was currently in or the one he was about to enter. Had she come back out to look for him? He didn't know. The eraser was a half a stroke away from eliminating the window all together. He had to make a decision.

Shane reflected on telling Emily to stay put in that painting and, in that instant, he knew. He jumped through the black window and within seconds it was erased. There was no going back now.

"Emily!" He shouted out, but there was no reply.

He was about to walk. Instead, he froze. A large pool was in front of him and it was filled with the craziest looking creatures. Were they fish? Or were they snakes? He had no idea.

Chapter Thirty-Two:
Disturbing DNA

What a relaxing night Jennifer had. Having all the kids with her had been wonderful and she felt such a burden lifted off her shoulders knowing that the house was safe from foreclosure. Now it as time to get the kids to school and daycare and then she would be off to work.

She stood with Clark at the door of the baby's daycare. She waited patiently for her turn so she could sign him in, hand over his bag, and hand him off to the worker. She smiled at him, softly touching his pouty lower lip with her finger. He was so precious. Finally, it was her turn. Jennifer hugged him tightly, kissed him on the forehead, and handed him over.

She made her way back to the car. Amanda and Christy were sitting in there, talking away with their arms all animated. A few minutes later, she was at school. She got out of the car and hugged the two girls, telling them to have a great day. "Be good. I love you."

"Love you too!" They called out and then turned around to run into school.

Jennifer jumped back in the car and made her way to work. She unlocked the lab door before entering into the room, which was dark aside from the light of the aquarium.

She turned the lights on and prepared for her day.

With everything she needed close by , she put on her lab coat and sat down in front of the microscope. There was a small light switch near the tube of the scope and she switched it on, lighting up the microscope lens. The sample she viewed showed on the computer screen monitor. There were several human DNA strains combined with what looked to be fish DNA. If it was mixed with human tissue, it'd have to be a fish that attacked humans. Jennifer looked over to the tank. The Chinese Snake Fish were aggressive, but would they do something like that? There wasn't a lot of research since they typically lived in very secluded places and enjoyed deep water. Whoever had gotten them into Caballo Lake had gone through some serious effort to do so. They didn't just get there by themselves. It would take extensive adaptation and that didn't just happen overnight.

As if it could read her thoughts, the snake-fish smashed aggressively into the glass of the tank, cracking it. At first, the water simply trickled out. Then the tank exploded, gushing water everywhere. The fish landed on the floor and began to flop around. Jennifer jumped out of her chair just in time. The fish wiggled its way underneath her desk where there was nothing but darkness. You couldn't see it. She moved away, hoping to get to a phone and call someone. She knew that she had to get to the lake where she'd been doing her research. Scaling over the makeshift filing cabinets and tables in order to stay as far away from the fish as possible, Jennifer grabbed her jacket, purse, and a megaphone before leaving.

She pulled up to the lake and swiftly made her way toward the boat, deciding to use the motor. There were people in the water swimming, enjoying themselves. She began to shout through the megaphone. "Everyone please clear the water. Clear the water now!" The people watched her, wondering if there was a good reason or if she was crazy. She kept shouting it out with urgency.

"Is there a problem?" One of the swimmers came up to Jennifer, trying to assess the situation.

"Yes, get to shore or get in the boat. The water is not safe for you to be in. I will take you back." Just then, a snake fish jumped high out of the water and dropped back into the pool, slapping the water as it landed. It made her heart race. She didn't know what was going to happen.

"What the hell?" the people stated, pointing to what they'd seen.

Jennifer just repeated herself. She stared at the swimmer. "Get in, now!"

This time the swimmer listened. She went back to the megaphone and began to call out orders. "Keep moving out of the water. One at a time. This lake is full of Chinese Snake Fish. They are a dangerous species. Walk calmly and don't stir up the water."

Finally, everyone was out of the water, staring at the mayhem unfolding in the lake. The fish had become more active, making their way to a spot in the water.

Jennifer sped over there, noticing the same truck was there from a few days back. It had not moved. She ran the boat up on shore and ran over to the truck, looking inside. The seats were empty. A pack of cigarettes sat on the dashboard, next to a picture of a man and woman hugging.

Suddenly, the police came swarming up, kicking people off the beach, and placing tape around the scene of the truck. She ran over to them, telling them her theory.

In addition to the police, there was also a marine biologist. Jennifer ran up to him next, eager to explain what she had discovered. The police were concerned with the crime and didn't realize they had no weapons that would eliminate the problem of the Chinese Snake Fish.

"How is it getting here?" the biologist asked.

"Someone is releasing them."

"Any idea how they'd get access to such a fish? It wouldn't be safe for them, first of all, but it's not easy to get into the territory where these fish commonly dwell," the biologist commented.

"I believe that whoever did this bred them, making their risk considerably less."

"Any research on how to address the problem?" the biologist asked Jennifer.

"That's where you come in…I hope," Jennifer said.

A damage control person came over. "I don't want people of this city to become aware of this situation. It could cost the mayor the election. Could this be a terrorist attack?"

"It's not for me to decide and keeping this a secret is the least of my concerns," Jennifer said. "We need to kill these fish, no matter what it takes."

The biologist spoke up. "We can poison the lake with Rowtinum. It will definitely kill every fish. Is there quick access to that?"

"We can get quick access," Jennifer said.

"Good," the biologist continued. "This should be done within days, right now if possible. There could be thousands of baby fish in that lake, ready to make their way into the city's water supply. Of course, that may have already happened."

The damage control person was standing there with his jaw dropped. "No. There has to be another way. A fishing season or something. We cannot have the environmentalists get a hold of this info or they will be protesting day and night."

"It's not going to be too easy for the mayor to win re-election when his townspeople are dead, is it?" Jennifer spat.

"I…uh…just be discreet, like I said." Then the

damage control person walked away, not wanting to hear anything else that had to be said.

The biologist was on his cell phone and Jennifer was on hers, trying to find enough Rowtinum to eliminate the fish population of the large lake. It wouldn't be easy, but it was necessary.

Chapter Thirty-Three:
The Devious

Tayyip drove Stacy's car to her usual spot at school to pick up the girls. He looked at himself in the mirror, pleased with how close he'd made his resemblance to hers. The sunglasses hid the shade of his eyes, which were different. The clueless Americans would have no idea though. They didn't pay close attention to the details of their daily lives. If they did, his plan wouldn't have been as easy as it had been thus far, despite having the most elaborate advanced technologies involved in it.

The small children began to depart for the day and Tayyip saw Amanda walking out to the car by herself. Christy wasn't there. She opened the passenger side door and got in the back. She sat there frowning, not speaking.

He watched as she looked for something in her backpack. She was occupied and didn't pay attention, but the traffic director did. She came up and tapped the window. "What seems to be the problem today?"

"Sorry."

"You know the routine," the woman said. The voice alarmed her and Amanda looked up, noticing the cream colored gloves, lipstick, and scarf.

"You seem different today. Are you alright?"

Not wanting to talk, Tayyip nodded his head, signaling he was okay and sped up the car. He merged into the traffic on the highway.

"There is a special place I want you to visit today," he finally said, trying to sound like Stacy.

Amanda looked at him with interest and dug into her backpack again. She pulled out her phone, trying to quietly dial a number. Despite her attempt, the buttons beeped loudly anyway. Tayyip looked in the mirror.

Tayyip said, "You should hang up the phone."

Amada said, "Sure."

"Let me have it." Amanda stared at her supposed aunt curiously and thought about it. She decided to hand it over.

Tayyip took the key out of the ignition and Amanda remained seated in the back. He looked at her, wondering why she wasn't getting out of the car. "I can't go inside there."

"You are here. Might as well."

"Take me where I am supposed to be."

"Come inside. Your mother will get you from here."

"Why are you dressed like that and why are you driving my aunt's car? You are not her."

"I'm a friend of both your mother and father."

"You knew my father?"

"Yes, I did. I knew him quite well."

"Let me make a phone call."

"You can come inside. Make the call from there."

He opened the door that led into the house, hoping he could find some food to entice the child with.

"I'm not hungry."

"Okay then. Suit yourself. I have a little friend I'd like you to meet. Her Daddy was friends with your parents."

* * * *

At about 5 p.m. Jennifer's phone rang. She'd been so busy that she hadn't had time to call anyone and let them know she'd be running late.

"Yes," she said, walking away. It was the daycare provider for Clark.

Her face paled and she hung up the phone." She went back to the biologist and said, "Something came up. I have to go."

"That's fine. We'll wrap up here. We've done all we can for the day."

"Thanks, see you tomorrow."

RONDER SCOTT

Jennifer ran to her car, thinking about how Stacy had probably gotten her days mixed up. Things had been crazy for both of them and even the most reliable of people could make a slip.

After apologizing, Jennifer took Clark and held him tightly. "Hi honey, how was your day?"

He kicked his little legs in response. She rushed to the car, putting him in the baby seat before making her way to Stacy's house. No one was home when she got there.

Stacy didn't answer her phone so she decided to call Dave.

"Hello," Dave said.

"Hey Dave, Jennifer. I am sorry to bother you, but have you seen Stacy today?"

"No, I'm not exactly welcomed around, especially after last night," he said.

Jennifer was about to ask a question, but it wasn't relevant at the moment. Where Stacy was at that minute was what was important.   "Well, I'm in front of your house right now. The car is not in the driveway. You have any idea where she may be?"

"I know Christy may have had to stay after school today. Maybe she's picking her up and then heading to get Clark," Dave offered.

"Um Dave, hold on." Jennifer clicked the button on her phone. "Hello Christy. Yes...no...are you sure? Okay I'll be there."

"Dave, hello. Yes something is wrong. She didn't pick up the baby or the girls. I'm worried. I'm going to get Christy and call the police, but can you meet us at my house later?"

"Sure."

"Okay, bye."

After Jennifer had Christy, she made her way back to Stacy's home and told Christy to wait in the car with the baby.

She walked into the house, calling out. "Stacy, you in here?" There was no answer, but the bathroom door was cracked open. There was a giant piece of glass covering the tub. She walked inside but didn't see anything out of line until she leaned over the glass.

There was Stacy, eyes wide open and obviously drown, gnawed at by the Chinese Snake Fish inside the tub with her. It was still moving, gasping for air.

Jennifer wanted to vomit, but she had no time. Something was wrong – deadly wrong – and she sensed danger for everyone. She charged back out to the car and shouted to Christy. "Amanda? Have you seen Amanda?"

"Not since second period."

"Oh my God," Jennifer said, jumping into the car. She took off quickly, squealing the tires and making the baby start crying. Christy was panicked, not sure what was going on either. She tried to comfort her little brother, but she wasn't very good at it since she was so scared herself.

She couldn't remember the drive, but Jennifer made it to her house, where Dave was already waiting. Christy ran out of the car and yelled, "Dad!" and jumped into his arms.

"The baby's in the car," Jennifer yelled as she ran into her house.

"Amanda? You in here honey?"

Dave walked to the entrance of the house and demanded to know what was going on.

"She's gone," was all Jennifer could say.

"Gone? What do you mean? Amanda's gone?"

"Stacy's gone – dead!"

"What?" Dave asked

"I have to find Amanda now," Jennifer said.

Jennifer grabbed her cell phone and pulled up the map that showed Amanda Koppell's location, which could always be traced by her cell phone. An address popped up on the screen: 525 Point Ridge Place. The lake was just a 6 mile drive from there. When she remembered that the deadly snake-fish were only recently released into the ecosystem, her thoughts turned to who was responsible for releasing those venomous predatory fish into the water stream. Someone who was out for blood.

Jennifer's stomach turned. She realized that house belonged to Stacy's boss. That was where they attended the party of well-rehearsed lies. Now everything was connecting. She was in a game and this game had her name written in blood. She would have assumed that Stacy was in on it if she weren't lying dead in her bathtub. Her best friend and sister-in-law was true until the end.

Realizing that Jennifer had led everyone into a trap was agonizing. She contemplated how she could be so willing to fall to death's mercy. Her head began to spin as she connected all the dots. This was solely one man's doing and one man's motivation. Those eyes; no wonder they looked so familiar. Images of a young, innocent boy taking his last breath flashed through her mind. Even those paintings on the wall made more sense. Everything was adding up, but at a high price. Why did her loved ones have to pay for her stalled and displaced memory?

She didn't have time to relive the nightmares though. She had to get there and figure out what was going on – play it smart. The man was obviously ruthless and out of control right now. She needed to save her daughter come hell or high water.

"Dave, I need your credit card."

"What? Why? No."

"It's life or death," Jennifer said.

He handed the card over. Jennifer whipped it into her purse. She pulled out a note pad, scribbling down some information.

"Dave, I have to go. Please send the police to this address. There's been a kidnapping. At your address, there is a death." Jennifer could barely choke the words out.

"What is this about?" Dave and Christy watched Jennifer's demeanor change. They saw how serious and panicked she was. She almost seemed delusional. She ignored the looks and handed the address to Dave.

He took the address. "Are you okay?"

"Please don't go back into your house tonight. Just stay here with the kids. Call the police and give them this information. Just do as I say please."

Jennifer took off, speeding toward the airport. When she got out of her car she thought she was having a hallucination. Two men on ropes were coming down from the sky.

"Jennifer Koppell," one said.

"Yes," she said, not sure what to do. She wanted to run into that airport, but she was frozen, thinking she had finally gone insane.

"I'm Agent O with the FBI. Please come with me. We can get you to your daughter."

"What?"

The other man, who identified himself as Agent Z, spoke next. "There's no time for questions now."

"She's in real trouble."

"We can get you there in ten minutes."

Jennifer was very aware this was like a science fiction movie, but she had to trust these men. She had to.

Not saying a word and trying to process things, Jennifer was lifted up into the air rapidly. She came down in the place she'd been at just a week before. Now it seemed so different...like a movie studio.

Then she was attached to another rope and lowered down into what seemed like nothing, but ended up being a place she definitely remembered. It was the property of Tayyip Nafisi. Jennifer walked across the lawn with the two agents behind her. Slowly, she made her way to a window. When she looked through the window, she saw Tayyip Nafisi standing there. How could she have been so stupid? She suddenly remembered the party with Stacy. He was George Sterling. Then she remembered the owner of the bank that tried to foreclose on her. He'd been watching her, stalking her. She had thought he was kind. Well, he wasn't. He was a monster.

Chapter Thirty-Four:
Finding Emily

Shane stood there, assessing the situation, not sure how he was going to make it past the water with the crazy creatures in it. They were jumping out of the water. He could hear their jaws snapping as they flew through the air before landing in the water once again.

There was a thin glass beam that went across the tank, but he didn't think he'd be able to cross it with his leg. Hell, he might be too heavy for it even if he didn't have a bum leg. What was he going to do?

Just then a motor started to buzz, causing Shane to look up. A door was sliding open from above, like it was in the ceiling and a wire cage was being lowered down. He watched it, almost losing his balance when one of the fish smacked his injured leg with its tail.

"Daddy!" It was Emily. Shane stared as she was lowered down in the cage.

"Oh my God, Em. Are you okay?"

"I'm scared Daddy, but I'm okay. There's someone else here with me too. She's scared, but she's smart."

"Who is that?" Shane asked.

"Her name is Amanda Koppell. The man who has us said that you know her parents."

"Who has you?" Shane asked, already planning his revenge.

"Tac…Tray…Tay…Tayyip something," Amanda said.

"Tayyip," Shane repeated.

"And who are the other girl's parents?"

"Her mom's name is Jennifer and she said her dad's name was Issac."

"Issac Rainnek," Shane said aloud. Then it registered with him. She was with Issac Rainnek and Jennifer Koppell's daughter.

Shane began to sweat, feeling every one of his nerves pulsating in his body. "Was the man's name Tayyip Nafisi, Em?"

"That's it," Emily said.

A calm and quiet voice sounded out from somewhere. Shane couldn't see anyone. It was through a speaker.

"Mr. Braff, you've put up quite the elaborate display of skills in my paintings. Have you enjoyed yourself?"

"You son of a bitch!" Shane shouted. "Let her go. It's me you have a problem with, not her."

"Well, it seems you had a problem with my family that one day. Do you remember that day? Does it haunt your thoughts?"

"We were mis-informed. It was tragic, but it was an error, not deliberate. This is deliberate, Tayyip. There's a huge difference."

"Surely you are not suggesting that your military ordered you to kill my son and wife."

"We didn't kill your wife."

"Her death was slow and painful. What you did that day did kill her. It just took years for it to happen."

"Come out here and deal with me personally if you're so tough," Shane said.

"Oh, I plan on watching you die, along with Jennifer Koppell," Tayyip said. "I'm going to make sure you get to watch me delighting in it too."

Shane turned back to Emily, who was listening to everything. Her eyes were wide open. She was clearly terrified. She stared below her, where she could see the aggressive fish jumping up, getting closer to her each time.

"Emily, don't look at them. Just stay calm. I'm coming to get you," Shane said.

"You're quite the hero. Touch the child and I'll drop the bottom of that cage open and give my precious fish an extra snack," Tayyip said.

Emily started to cry and Shane looked at his baby,

desperate to hold her and let her know that everything would be alright. She would be fine.

Chapter Thirty-Five:
Two Tayyip's

Jennifer stared with a horrific feeling in her gut. There sat Tayyip, listening to classical music and sipping from a small mug. He wore a black sweater over a gray button down shirt and a black tie. He was polished to the nines, looking very refined for an obvious mad man.

Suddenly, he got up and began to walk down the long hallway. Jennifer watched him through the window, wanting to go in and annihilate him, but knowing she had to keep her cool. So many thoughts were flooding into her mind, distracting her.

Tayyip entered a room where Jennifer couldn't see him. She began to walk around the house, hoping she could watch him through a different window. The two FBI agents remained in the distance. They knew Jennifer was highly qualified. The plan was to get the kids and Shane Braff out of the house. They would lift them out of the painting and get them back to the safety of the studio – in the real world in real time. Jennifer would go last.

As Tayyip walked into the room, he was joined by another man. He'd just gotten done talking into a speaker phone and was smiling, watching Emily dangling in a cage above the Chinese Snake Fish while her father watched her in agony.

Tayyip walked over to the man, someone dressed very stately – you could even say presidential – and spoke animatedly. "I want to be paid cash like we initially agreed. Got it?"

"Think about it, Gregory. How do you think you are going to get out of here with all that money and still keep it? I promise you the money will be sitting in an account for you as soon as you get out of jail."

The fake Tayyip, also known as Gregory, said, "I'm having second thoughts about this."

"They can't keep you more than six months. It is brilliant. The only thing they can hold you for is interrupting the network and the network will be eating out of your hands. They won't press charges because this stunt pulled in unprecedented ratings for them. You both win. You will be slapped with a fine and no more than a few months in jail. There will be two million dollars waiting for you when you get out. Naturally, that only happens if you keep your mouth closed through everything. I promise you, I will make sure nothing happens to you ever."

Jennifer had found the window where Tayyip was, but, as she watched the two men interact, she knew something was definitely awry. The man who looked like Tayyip Nafisi had different body posture and mannerisms than the actual Tayyip did. The other man, who looked like the President of the United States, however, had Tayyip's exact mannerisms, despite not looking like him. *A switch,* Jennifer thought. *But why?*

The actor Tayyip Nafisi's face was tense. He looked at the computer screen which had an account on it with his name in it. There was a large dollar amount entered, ready to have a deposit transfer from another. The mouse clicker was in Tayyip's right hand and the cursor blinking over the *submit* button. The actor Tayyip finally nodded and the button was clicked.

Afterward, Tayyip reached for a piece of paper on the desk, sliding it across for his impersonator to sign. He signed it and put the paper securely inside his briefcase. They shook hands and the fake President walked away, leaving the actor standing there with his hands in his pockets. The fake Tayyip stared at the floor, not sure where to look and certainly how to feel.

Tayyip left his house and made his way toward the Lincoln Town Car limousine, one that was worthy of the most notable dignitaries, and briefly glanced around. He saw four men standing next to their motorcycles, dressed in black sweaters, slacks, and shoes. They all wore helmets, keeping their facial features a mystery.

The door to the limo opened up and the chauffer stood there, waiting with a smile. "Good evening, sir."

Tayyip nodded.

Chapter Thirty-Six:
Remains

"I have to go in now to get Amanda."

"We received word that others are in there too," Agent Z said.

"Who?"

"Shane Braff and his daughter, Emily," Agent Z replied.

"Shane Braff?" Jennifer was shocked. Then she recalled thinking she saw him on that day in Rhode Island at the studio. She must have really seen him and not just imagined it.

Shane was highly capable though. She had to worry about Amanda. That was her priority. She heard strange noises coming from inside the walls. The bricks slid out of place, leaving space for killing machines to lock and load on their targets. In the next instant, gunfire blasted, ricocheting in the open space. Bullets smashed into the agent's bulletproof vest, sending him searching for cover. A block on the wall opened up, revealing what was behind it. Jennifer could see the silver paneling and knew immediately the wall was protected.

Jennifer climbed inside the opening. The panel facing the gunfire came down before any of the bullets could hit her. She saw the bullets indent and breathed in a sigh of relief. She looked up cautiously, not wanting to risk rising to more bullets but she knew she had to push her way out of there and keep moving. She lifted her legs to her breasts, tucking her knees close to her. Turning her body, she kicked the wall, hoping she could break through to the other side. She could feel the sharp chards of glass scratching her skin from the other side, but she didn't care. She had to get to Amanda and save her. She had no idea what she was up against, but failure wasn't an option.

She made a dent in the wall big enough to climb through. The former soldier found herself in an empty dark room. She went to the door, noticing the lava red door knob on it. If she touched it, she knew she would suffer severe burns. She took off her shirt and wrapped her hand before touching the door, hoping it wasn't locked and that she'd be able to turn the knob quickly. When she pulled the door, it took everything in her not to let go, but she got the door open.

Once in the hallway, there was no sign of gunfire, a single person, or the Agents sent there to rescue her. She didn't even know if they made it out alive, but she was standing and she knew every moment counted. She picked herself up and brushed off the debris, feeling the painful sting in her hand. Adrenaline rushed through her body like lighting and provided enough 'juice' for her to stay focused on the mission at hand.

Moving door to door, every door was locked aside from one. She slowly opened the door and poked her head around the corner. She felt so nervous and anxious.

She wished she had a gun, but she'd stopped carrying one despite having a conceal and carry permit. Jennifer had lost confidence in herself over the past years and didn't trust her instincts or behavior enough.

The lights were off, but, in the shadows, was a perfectly made bed, vanity, and a mirror with a chair tucked underneath. As Jennifer walked slowly through the room she saw that everything was in place. Then she spotted the silver box glimmering in the pale light and walked over to it.

The box looked like a casket to her; she felt her nose starting to tingle, making her want to sneeze. She held her breath, not wanting to make any noises and slowly walked closer to the box, wondering what it was about.

She leaned down, slowly lifting the heavy silver lid up to look inside. A huge whiff of a vile and pungent odor came out of it. Jennifer went pale, wanting to scream. She was staring at a dead body, partially decomposed, but the face was intact enough for her to tell exactly who it was. It was Faridah Nafisi, Tayyip's wife. Lying across her chest was a picture of her son, Hossien, who'd died that fateful day at this house nearly four years ago.

Jennifer slammed the lid shut. She knew she had to act quickly. Nothing short of making anybody involved in that day suffer was on Tayyip's mind. That's why Shane was here too. She had to find Amanda. But where? The house seemed so quiet and all the doors were locked. If she opened up a door she had no idea if she'd end up in a different painting or if some trap would go off.

Jennifer knew that she had to calm her thoughts in order to make the smartest choices. She had to return to combat mode, a place she'd tried to avoid at all costs unless she was training Amanda in her back yard. She was also aware of how much that had cost her. If she'd kept that sharp edge she'd always had, she would have realized that Tayyip Nafisi was back in her life and she could have saved Stacy.

Suddenly, tears sprung to Jennifer's eyes. She'd managed to put Stacy out of her mind, but the memories of what she'd seen had snuck out. The evil imagery Tayyip created flashed through her mind all at once. He'd had a well thought out and calculated plan, one that was funded by the US government. They'd given him a hefty pay-off and he seemingly used every cent of it to extract his revenge on those who had hurt him most. Jennifer was pained by the fact that she'd been a part of it. She'd known it was wrong to let the scene unfold the way it had at the time, but she hadn't said anything. She pressed her body against that wall and let it happen, too afraid to defy orders.

Her thoughts were forced to drift back to the present situation. Jennifer thought about Issac and what he would do. He would have protected her and made the danger go away. However, the cards fell into her hands and she needed to start thinking like Tayyip if she wanted to win.

"Don't be hesitant...that's what he wants." She heard Issac's voice in her mind, but she was there alone to face her demons. She stood up and began to search the room, hoping to find something that would give her a clue. There was a reason, other than seeing the corpse of his wife, that Tayyip had wanted Jennifer to go into this room. She had to figure out what it was.

Chapter Thirty-Seven:
Inherited Intelligence

Amanda stared as Emily came back up through the floor in the metal cage she'd been in. Her face was pale and she looked so frightened. The cage door automatically opened. She climbed out as quickly as she could. She did not even want to think about getting back in there.

"What happened?" Amanda asked.

"My dad was there. He couldn't get to me though. I know he'll find a way."

"That's good. My mom's going to be coming – I just know it and your dad is here. They'll get us out of here."

"We need to try to figure a way out ourselves too. I know this is a painting, but from what I can remember at the meeting we had that day there is a way out of each painting. Finding it isn't easy, but it's there."

"That's not how our meeting went at all," Amanda said. "I couldn't even recall being in Rhode Island until I got to this house. I knew we'd gone there, but it was kind of like we forgot. We just went on living our life."

"I'd told Daddy that I thought the paintings fed off our emotions, using our likely responses against us." Emily looked at Amanda, wishing she could have met her under different circumstances. They were very different, but kind of the same in their toughness. Maybe they had to be because they'd both lost a parent. Only Emily had lost her mom in a mysterious car accident. She wasn't in the military.

"I hope not. What if that means something happens to my mom? I couldn't handle that," Amanda said.

Suddenly Emily ran over by the cage, needing to see if she could see her Dad. If she could, she'd know he had a plan. She peered down into the room she'd been lowered. She saw her Dad standing there, looking like he was going to walk across the glass beam to get to a door that had suddenly appeared on the other side.

"No Daddy!" She yelled it, but he couldn't hear her. She didn't know why - he wasn't that far away, but he couldn't.

Suddenly there was a loud banging and the girls jumped, trying to figure out what it was.

"Where did that come from?" Emily asked.

"The walls maybe," Amanda said. They looked around and there was a loud thump again. Suddenly some white powder fell on both of their heads and they looked up. Amanda whispered, "The ceiling."

"Quick, grab the blanket over there to cover our heads. We don't know what's going to come through there," Emily said.

"Mom's always told me to hide under the sturdiest thing if you think something might fall on you...to protect you, you know."

"There's nothing in here though," Emily replied.

"Then let's stand with our backs to the wall, straight as can be, and cover our heads with the blanket. It's the best idea," Amanda said.

The two went to press their bodies against the wall of the room, but as they did, they could feel a violent thrashing coming from behind the wall. They took a step forward, not so worried about the ceiling anymore and watched as the walls lowered themselves, revealing a large swarm of scary creatures.

"Those are the Chinese Snake Fish my mom's been working with," Amanda said.

"Are they violent?" Emily asked, too afraid to take her eyes off of them.

"I think so," Amanda said. Just then, one of them smashed into the glass and they could hear a cracking noise, although they couldn't see it. Then, a few feet away in the corner, they saw a small trickle of water start to go onto the floor.

The two girls, not knowing what else they could do, screamed. They screamed so loud, knowing that what was about to happen was something they couldn't outsmart.

Chapter Thirty-Eight:
The Trap

Jennifer stopped rummaging the room and her heart began racing. She heard noise and it was coming from below her. Then there was a scream, one that she would recognize anywhere. The last time she'd heard it was when her daughter saw the neighbor's dog get run over.

"Amanda!" Jennifer began shouting, hoping to find out where the noise was coming from. The screams continued on though and there was no answer. Jennifer ran around the room, putting her ear to every wall, but she heard nothing. Then she suddenly knelt down on the floor and heard it coming from there.

"Oh my God! She's underneath me," Jennifer said. She started to ransack the tidy room and look for anything that was weighty enough that it could be used to bust open the floor. She slid open the closet doors so fast that she knocked one off its track. She found that the closet was empty except for two things: a sledgehammer and a vacuum core drilling rig. Had Tayyip really been able to plan out her every move that well? It was a chilling thought, but she had no option aside from saving Amanda, even if Tayyip knew she was going to do it. She'd just have to be resourceful.

Take a deep breath, Jennifer thought. She began smashing it the floor with the sledgehammer, hoping to break through. She pounded for all she was worth, swinging that sledgehammer over her head and smashing it down into the floor, letting out all her aggressions and desperation on it.

She began to yell Amanda's name repeatedly. Then what she heard was music to her ears. It was Amanda yelling back.

"Mom! Hurry!"

"Stay calm and cover your heads. I don't know how much of this is going to fall down, okay?"

"Okay. Just hurry. Water's leaking in and those snake-fish things are thrashing at the tank, trying to get out. I'm with Emily. You've got to hurry, Mom!"

Jennifer was more frantic than ever, busting through the cement was not working she went back to the closet and pulled out the XXL drill. She thought at first Tayyip rigged the power not to work but she tried the lights and one bulb flashed on then shot out instantly. She took the plug and put it into the wall, pressing the button and it powered up. Her heart fell, thinking of all the time she wasted second guessing herself and trying to outthink Tayyip.

"Is Shane there?"

"He's trapped by some fish in a layer below us," Emily called out.

"Okay girls. Stay calm. I'm almost there," Jennifer said. Her hand was throbbing so much that it was hard to keep a good grasp on the drill and she could feel her muscles tensing up, barely able to move it back and forth.

Some of the fish thrashed against the tank again and the girls screamed. Jennifer knew she had to keep them thinking.

"Do you see anything long in the room?" Jennifer asked.

"No," Amanda said. "It's nearly empty. All we have is us and this blanket."

"Do you have a jacket or a hoodie on? Anything like that?" Jennifer asked.

"I have a hoodie on," Emily called out.

"I don't have anything, Mom. It was a really nice day when it started."

It was almost as if the word nice agitated the fish further. They began to get more violent, thrashing about.

"Tie the hoodie to the blanket in as tight a knot as you can. Try to make a makeshift rope out of that, okay?"

"Okay," Amanda said. Emily took off the hoodie she'd been wearing before running over to see if she could see her Dad below.

"Daddy!"

Shane looked up, but didn't respond. He was staring

where Emily was, but it was as if he didn't see her.

Emily turned to Amanda. "Do you think we should get in this cage? At least if those things get out they can't get to us."

"Let me ask Mom," she said. Amanda stared up at the ceiling, able to tell the exact spot that Jennifer was pounding on. "There's a cage in here. Should we go in there, Mom?"

"Do you think the tanks will hold out?" Jennifer called out.

Amanda could barely choke out a no. The water had started to flow so fast that their sneakers were completely soaked through. The two girls went to the small cage and squeezed in, having no room to move around at all. They couldn't even stand up.

Jennifer kept pounding with the drill. Suddenly, she broke through the floor. She knelt down and stared in horror. She saw Amanda and Emily huddled together in that small cage without a lot of options to help them.

"Is your dad doing anything below, Emily?" Jennifer asked.

"He can't hear me. I can see him though."

"Let me see what I can find up here," Jennifer said. She ran away, rummaging the room for a rope or something. She couldn't find one so she quickly ripped the sheets off the bed. They were silk. It would make it very tough for someone to hold on to them, but it was her only choice.

She came back to the hole and began to call out instructions just as the cage which the girls were in spiraled downward, going completely out of sight except for the chain which held it to the fastener in the ceiling. Frantic, she found the heaviest thing she could, the handle on the silver box which held Faridah's remains, and tied the sheet to it, hoping it would hold her as she scaled down into that room.

Chapter Thirty-Nine:
The Ultimate Sacrifice

Shane was making his way across the fragile beam, trying to remain as slow and steady as possible. He breathed in, pausing every time a jolt of pain rattled his body. His concentration was suddenly broken by the screams coming from above him. He looked up and saw the cage that Emily had been in earlier plummeting down right above him.

He started to move quickly, hoping to get out of the way, but he stumbled, falling down to his knee. One of the creatures in the tank jumped up into the air and flew over his head, landing with a forceful impact against the cage. It had stopped just above Shane and he couldn't stand up now.

"Daddy!" Emily screamed out.

"I'm here, hon. I'm here."

"Help us!"

"I'm trying. I have to find a way to slide out. I can't stand up. The cage is close. I need you to do me a favor though," Shane said. "Stay calm and don't scream. I think it agitates these things more...whatever they are."

"They're Chinese Snake Fish," Emily said. "Amanda's mom has been studying them. She's here."

Shane began to use his one good leg to push

backward on the beam, hoping to clear the cage. A smaller one of the fish flew up and attached itself to his arm. He bit down on his teeth to stop from screaming. He reached over with his one good arm and tried to pry it off. Its teeth were really sunk into him, but he squeezed just below the jaw line as hard as he could until it finally released its grip. He tossed it far away, but his arm was bleeding, sending a slow trickle of red blood into the water. All of the fish began to swarm around it, hungry for more and instinctually knowing that a feast of flesh was somewhere close by.

Just two more pushes and you'll have cleared it, Shane thought. He grimaced the entire time, becoming increasingly distracted by all the pain. Another fish had bit onto his pant leg and he couldn't reach it to get it off. It easily went through the thick jean material and planted in his leg – the same one that had already been shot.

He looked up and saw Amanda and Emily watching him. They knew what was going on, tears streamed down their eyes. The last thing Shane needed was for them to be any more scared than they already were. They had to maintain calm heads so they could figure a way to get out of there. Then, the first chance he could, Shane would take that Tayyip Nafisi and shred him apart, no matter what the consequences.

Just as Shane stood up, a soft voice came from above. He looked up and so did Emily and Amanda. It was Jennifer.

Shane and Jennifer looked at each other briefly,

knowing that they'd have to work together one last time to save their children. After that day, the one that happened at this very house, their once tight unit had fallen apart. Each of them had their own demons from what they experienced and, as a result, they were not able to work with each other the way they once had. Seeing their teammates for the mission only brought back painful memories and reminders of what everyone lost that day.

The cage moved up slowly and Shane reached out to hold it as steady as he could so it wouldn't rock. Then it started to slow down and a creaking noise, not unlike an old house on a windy day, started to sound out from above.

Hanging on as tightly as he could, Shane was about six feet away from the beam of glass below him that he'd been crossing. It wouldn't be an easy jump to make, but he was clearly too heavy to be hoisted up at the same time as the girls.

Jennifer's voice was now frantic, shouting from the room above. "It's getting ready to snap!"

Shane looked up and then looked down. He knew what he had to do at that moment and there was not another second to spare, or even to debate it.

"Emily, I love you so much. I know you'll always make me proud!" He stared up at her beautiful frightened eyes and winked, like always liked to do to her. Then he shouted again. "Jennifer! Watch over my daughter and kill the bastard!"

Shane released his grip on the bar and his heavy body fell quickly.

"No! Daddy!" Emily was screaming.

He landed on the beam straight, keeping his balance. However, there was a crack in the beam and it began to move quickly. Within seconds, it shattered the beam and Shane went plummeting into the depths of the tank of fish. As he went down he could hear Emily screaming, "I love you, Daddy! No!"

In an instant the fish began to swarm on Shane's body, satisfied to finally get to eat the flesh that had been taunting them. As they surrounded his large body you could see no more signs of Shane, only bright red seeping out into the water, being swirled around by the aggressive tails of the snake-fish as they flailed about, making sure they each got their share of the flesh.

Chapter Forty:
The Last Hope

The cage continued to move upward slowly, making so much noise. Eventually it just jerked to a stop, leaving Amanda and Emily dangling about five feet below the place they needed to be. Neither knew what to do. It was too gruesome to look down. Emily was just staring, in shock at what she'd just seen happen to her dad, not sure how to process anything.

Jennifer came to the edge. "Okay girls. Listen up. We don't have much time. The chain is going to snap so I need you to do as I say and act quickly. Got it?"

"Yes, Mom," Amanda said. She realized that all that training that her mom had always had her do in the backyard seemed so ridiculous at the time, like something that would never be used, but now she had to use it and she had to keep her head.

Amanda looked to Emily, who was shaking so uncontrollably that the cage was starting to sway. "You've got to stay calm and listen to my mom, okay?"

Emily shook her head slightly.

Jennifer called out to the girls, telling them what they had to do. "I need you to open the door to that cage and one of you needs to climb on the top of it. I am going to toss something down to pull you up. You'll need to come out one at a time to do this. Tie the sheet around your waist tightly and hold on to it tightly. Got it?"

Amanda nodded yes. She turned to look at Emily and said, "You go first, okay?"

Emily shook her head no, but Amanda insisted. "You need to get out of here. It's too much down here for you. It makes the most sense."

Jennifer could hear her daughter talking, surprised at her maturity. It made her realize just how much she'd had to grow up to deal with her mother's emotional problems over the past years.

Amanda leaned over slowly and unlatched the door to the cage. It swung open. She moved to the side as much as she could so Emily could get over to it.

"You'll be fine," Amanda said. Emily crawled over and hesitated in front of the open door, not ready to go out of it. "You can do it, Emily. You can do it."

Emily slowly turned her body backward, grasping the outside of the cage just above the door opening and she looked at Amanda, who smiled at her. "Good job. You're doing great, Emily."

She slowly made her way up and her entire body was outside the cage now. Her feet were resting on the bottom of it and she breathed in deeply and began to climb up the cage like it was a ladder.

The cage started to sway back and forth a bit and Emily paused, hoping that would steady it. There was a loud noise, making her realize that the chain was getting weaker. She knew she had to focus on what was happening now. Not what she'd just seen.

Emily used all her strength to climb on top of the cage. The second she was there, Jennifer tossed down the sheet and Emily tied it around her waist. She made her way up slowly, staring up at the opening above her. She could only see the bottom of Jennifer's feet as she used them for leverage to help her tug her up more quickly.

Emily's head popped through the hole and Jennifer gave one last tug, sending her body flopping up onto the floor. Without a minute to spare, she untied the rope from her waist and tossed it back down. To her surprise, Amanda was already on top of the cage, making her heart skip a beat.

"You ready?" Jennifer called out.

"Ready, Mom," Amanda said. The makeshift rope was tossed down to her. She started to wrap it around her waist when, all of a sudden, the chain snapped. The cage dropped from right under her feet.

Amanda was hanging on to the edge of the sheet, trying to move her hands up so she had more room.

"Amanda! Wrap it around your hands," Jennifer screamed.

"I'm trying," Amanda shouted. She was swaying about and couldn't help but look down. Her dangling body had captured the Chinese Snake Fish's attention and they were flying through the air and coming dangerously close to the bottom of her feet.

"Start pulling me up, Mom," Amanda shouted.

"You don't have a good enough grip," Jennifer said.

"Trust me." That was Amanda's reply and Jennifer knew she had no reason not to. She began to tug on the makeshift rope, pulling her up. Suddenly, it became a bit easier. She turned her head and saw Emily behind her, pulling as hard as she could, staring straight ahead. It was almost like she was in a trance, but she was doing the best she could to help.

Amanda had slowly made her way up the sheet that was acting as a rope. She managed to get one of her hands wrapped around it, but not the other one. Jennifer was pulling as fast as she could and Amanda was trying to help, but she kept slipping downward because of the silky material.

With one last desperate tug, Jennifer got Amanda close enough to where she could grab her hands in hers. She found a reserve of strength that she didn't know she had left and began to pull her upward. Amanda's head finally made it through the hole. As Jennifer tried to pull her daughter into the room with her, one of Amanda's hands slipped out of her sweaty grasp. The girl was dangling by one arm.

Then, Emily was there leaning over the edge, holding

out her hands. Amanda looked to her and tried to reach her, but she was too far away. Emily leaned further down into the hole and Amanda tried again. This time they reached each other and Emily started to move backward. With Jennifer and Emily tugging with all their might, Amanda finally made it through the hole, landing on the ground. There had never been three more relieved faces.

Jennifer dove over to Amanda, who was still lying down and hugged her like crazy, kissing her entire face. Then the tears started to flow. First it was from Jennifer, then Amanda.

Emily didn't cry, but she couldn't take her eyes off of what she saw. It wasn't the emotional reunion of Jennifer and Amanda though. It was the dead body that had fallen out of the silver box on the floor.

Now they had to get up to the next level, the one that Jennifer had scaled down from. It was slow and painful, but they all did it, mustering their courage and strength. They had a determination to survive.

Jennifer was the last one up and when she finally got up there she saw Amanda and Emil staring at something.

"You girls turn away. You don't need to see that," she said.

Amanda and Emily did as she said. Wanting to vomit herself, Jennifer walked over to the box because she noticed something odd. The back of the silver box had opened up, revealing a secret compartment. There were wads of money in there and some pads with stickers wrapped in plastic.

Jennifer grabbed the information from the box. She knew it was important, but wasn't sure why. She'd take it, but now they had to get out and get back to the FBI agents that were waiting outside. It was time to leave this painting for good.

Then Jennifer realized that she didn't know for certain that Tayyip Nafisi or whomever she'd seen that looked like him was captured or not. Even after all this, she couldn't just assume that he had nothing else planned. What more could he take away though?

"Stay behind me girls and keep a look-out for everything. We're going to leave through the front door, okay?"

"Okay," they said. The two held hands and looked around at everything as they followed closely behind Jennifer. She had no weapon aside from the sledgehammer she'd used earlier, but she held it up, ready to unleash it on anyone that tried to do any more damage than what had already been done.

The house was completely silent and Jennifer looked through a sidelight on the front door before she opened it. She flicked the front porch light on and off a few times, signaling that they were coming out.

"Okay girls. It's safe," Jennifer said.

The three walked out of the house and made their way to the men sent to protect them, the FBI who were secured in their harnesses and waiting to take everyone back to the real world before permanently sealing off the land of paintings that had caught them, devastating their lives in the cruelest of ways. She didn't see Agent O or Z anywhere in sight.

"We can't leave here without them." Jennifer said.

"Don't worry about them. They were taken out of the painting already. They are being seen by doctors as we speak. It's your turn now, hang on tight. We got you."

"I'm very sorry about your dad, Emily. He was a strong man," Jennifer said, embracing Emily. She barely moved her head, but she couldn't stop the tears from flowing down her cheeks again.

Jennifer put her hand on Emily's shoulder. "I'll be here to do whatever it takes, Emily. I promise." Then Jennifer turned back to the agents. "Did you get him?"

"Nafisi disappeared, but we found a credible threat that he was pursuing the president. The president is on his way into hiding right now."

Jennifer didn't want to reveal her thoughts. The man was on the loose and that meant that no one had any assurance that they'd be safe. Perhaps that's what he wanted, but she suspected that he believed they'd all be dead. His time to carry out the plan to completion had simply expired...for now.

Jennifer watched as Amanda and Emily made their way back up to the studios and looked around the premises, trying to make sense of it all. What a talented man Tayyip Nafisi was. She had to give him credit for that. She also couldn't blame him for his hatred of her either, of anyone that was involved in that fateful day. It had changed everyone's lives forever. If only she would have stood up for what was right that day. If only...

Chapter Forty-One:
Some How, Some Way

The FBI was acting quickly, ensuring that they got the President to a safe location just in case Tayyip Nafisi was ready to act out on his threat to eliminate him. What he'd done to the members of the military squadron that had took him into custody that one day showed he was a highly intelligent and extremely emotionally motivated man, capable of doing anything if he justified it to be in the name of the life he lost.

At the White House, the President was being hustled out through the tunnels underneath. However, already on the road in Washington D.C. was a motorcade that was supported by full FBI personnel and carrying the official seal of the President of the United States on the sides of its Lincoln Town Car Limousine.

Inside of it, Tayyip Nafisi sat, feeling every bit as presidential as he looked. There was an agent on one side of him and two across from him. They'd all worked with the real president extensively over the past three years he'd been in office and had no clue that he was not the real deal. He smiled, thinking of his genius. There clearly was no American that could outsmart him from the way it appeared. In the end, Jennifer Koppell and Shane Braff had proven they could not either. Neither had seen their demise coming and that was what made it good drama. It was highly unpredictable.

They pulled up into the private presidential hangar at

the airport and armed guards and FBI personal were everywhere, preparing for the jet to take off. Naturally he would not be flying Air Force One that day, as that was for dignitary trips, not trips that would take him into hiding. Yet, it was equipped with the best of technology, not able to be tracked by any radar, missile detection system, or other technology. Whatever any country had invented, Tayyip had created a way to counter the effectiveness of it when it came to tracking and self defense. Of course none of those countries knew that at the moment, but they would soon enough.

Naturally, Tayyip had ensured that the press was present although it was secret. Leaks of that nature were his perverse little twist on his abilities to get people to see what he wanted them to see, not what actually was.

Fastening his suit jacket, Tayyip prepared to get out of the limousine and make his way to the jet. One of the agents got out first, followed by him. He smiled and waved to the press as they clicked their pictures of him, and called out for quotes. He said nothing to them, but carried out every mannerism that the pompous leader of the free world had, making words hardly necessary.

There were six armed guards by the steps of the jet. They were there to ensure nothing went wrong as their boss prepared to leave. Those six men were the only ones who knew who they were working for in that moment.

Once on the jet, Tayyip finally spoke freely. He looked at the Air Force Captain, who was the pilot for the jet and smiled. "You are free to go. Thank you."

"I'm the only one that can fly this jet, sir."

"That simply isn't true."

The pilot looked at Tayyip and then at the men. He realized something was wrong and he knew that he couldn't abandon the jet. Seeing his suspicion, Tayyip turned to one of his men.

"Clearly we cannot show kindness and let the man go. Take care of that for me please."

The pilot dodged toward the steps that led into the jet, but the door had already been closed. A man came up behind him and hit him on the head with the handle of his gun and the pilot collapsed.

"What shall we do with him, sir?" the one guard asked.

"Oh, just keep him out of my sight until we're high above. Then you can eject him out into the ocean if you like. It really doesn't matter."

"Yes, sir."

The new pilot took over, punching in the coordinates for the true destination. This bunker and hide-out certainly weren't in the Nevada desert. They were a place that was a bit more appealing, a place where Tayyip would be surrounded with abundant amounts of greenery and sparkling blue water in which to rejuvenate and start a new life.

The engines fired up on the jet and Tayyip sat in the center, buckled his belt, and enjoyed the lavish luxury of the presidential jet. It really was of good taste. He'd have to recall that for when he got his own private jet.

He turned on the television as they were taking off and it immediately captured his attention. A reporter was talking animatedly and the location she was at was one very familiar – it was the outside of the building where Painting, Inc. was located.

> *A dangerous man is on the loose. The authorities believe he may have already fled the country, but if you see him make sure to stay away and call the FBI hotline immediately. Do not approach him.*

A picture of Tayyip's face showed up on the television. He frowned, not at all pleased that they used such an old photograph. Then the reporter continued talking.

> *Three people are confirmed dead within the past twenty-four hours and their names are not being released yet. As you know, this started during the interruption of the Super Bowl...*

The words the reporter said caught Tayyip off guard. Three were reported dead. There should have been four. He knew that Stacy Fave and Dan Markel had died. So...that meant that either Jennifer Koppell or Shane

Braff were still alive. Perhaps both if one of their children died.

Standing up and walking to a compartment in the back of the jet, Tayyip grabbed an orange jumpsuit and baseball hat, that like which the airport workers wore on the tarmac, and slid it on over his suit. His work was not done quite yet, but it would be in a short amount of time. No matter what obstacles came his way, Tayyip knew that he would always be a few steps ahead of any real threats to his plans.

There was a small trap door in the bottom of the jet. He opened it up and connected the small ladder rope that attached to it and slid down, hiding his body behind one of the wheels of the jet as it began to make its way down the tarmac toward the runway.

He jumped on the ground and easily blended in with all the workers. He watched as the jet made it to the runway and began to take off, making its way into the dark sky at full speed.

Seconds after the jet was off, Tayyip got to witness another event. This one he hadn't planned on seeing, but it would be entertaining nonetheless. He watched as the real President and his motorcade arrived at the airport, leading to instant confusion and disarray. Yes, it was brilliant to watch and it made him smile brightly. How long would it take them to realize that their jet had been hijacked by Tayyip Nafisi and eventually learn that he wasn't even on it? Well, it mattered not. All Tayyip knew was that would delight in finishing what he started and then approaching the most powerful leaders in the world with the technology that they could either buy and be more dominant with, or reject and experience what it is like to be dominated. The choice was theirs to make.

Epilogue

Jennifer stood at the open grave, staring down into the hole, and feeling such sorrow at the loss of one of the best people she'd ever known. Behind her were Amanda and Emily; to the side were Dave, Clark, and Christy. Many others were there, but Jennifer didn't turn around, not wanting to make eye contact with anyone or expose her pain. She didn't know how she would manage what lied ahead of her, but she knew she had to. Someone she'd grown stronger from all the adversity and pain of the past days. Nothing would be the same again. This was particularly true in her heart.

The weather for Stacy's burial was nice, the type of day that usually beckoned her to 'play some hookie.' The minister spoke, bringing out tearful responses in everyone in attendance accept Jennifer. She couldn't cry. She was cried out. However, much to her surprise every word the minister said evoked anger in her. She knew she'd never be able to sleep until she met the man who'd been responsible for these unnecessary deaths face to face. She didn't know how long it would take to find Tayyip Nafisi or where he was, but she'd never stop trying. She also realized he may just seek her out again, like he did this past time. She wouldn't be so blind as to not see it though.

The service ended and Jennifer walked away with everyone else. The intensity of the day had her nerves on high alert. Before she got into the limousine with Dave and all the kids, she turned around to look at Stacy's grave. The cemetery worker was already there, starting to pile dirt into the hole. Jennifer paused briefly, thinking about how someone could do such a job. They had to have nerves of steel. As if he knew he was being watched by her, the guy turned around and smiled at Jennifer before getting back to digging.

"Come on, Mom," Amanda said.

Jennifer turned and got into the limousine and it pulled away, making its way to the restaurant for a meal in Stacy's honor. For some reason Jennifer turned around again and stared at the grave one more time. The man was gone and someone else was walking up to it with a shovel.

"Stop!" Jennifer yelled.

"What is it?" Dave asked.

She didn't answer. She just opened the door and ran to the grave.

"Where's the guy who was just here filling in the grave?" Jennifer asked.

The man, who obviously sensed her urgency, assumed it was about the death. "I'm sorry, ma'am. I'm the only with this job here."

"Thank you," Jennifer replied and she walked away, going back to the limousine. She mumbled under her breath. *He didn't waste much time, did he?*